Heather Grovet

REVIEW AND HERALD® PUBLISHING ASSOCIATION
HAGERSTOWN, MD 21740

The author assumes full responsibility for the accuracy of all facts and
quotations as cited in this book.

This book was
Edited by Jeannette R. Johnson
Cover illustration by Ron Bell
Cover design by Pierce Creative/Matt Pierce
Typeset: 13/16 Goudy Old Style

PRINTED IN U.S.A.

07 06 05 04 03   5 4 3 2 1

R&H Cataloging Service
Grovet, Heather Marie, 1963-
    Sarah Lee and a mule named Maybe.

    I. Title.

                813.6

ISBN 0-8280-1725-5

Dedication

To the world's greatest grandparents,
my grandma and grandpa Rawluk.

I love you!

Contents

1

The Endurance Race

I was roasting! Drops of sweat trickled off my fore-head and down my neck. My riding helmet was plastered to my long, brown hair, and my shirt clung to my back. I gathered the reins and glanced at my watch. It was almost 1:00 p.m., which meant Maybe and I had been racing for four hours now.

I was riding my big gray mule, Maybe, in a 30-mile endurance ride. My mom and her horse, El Sheba, were in the same race, except they were racing for 50 miles.

In an endurance race all the competitors start at the same time, but soon they're spread out on the trail. Some beginning racers start out too fast and can't finish the race because they're too exhausted. Some riders go too slow and don't complete the race within the allowed time.

Maybe and I started endurance racing last year, and we seem to be improving all the time. Mom says that Maybe's getting fitter and I'm getting smarter.

Dad says *I'm* getting fitter and *Maybe's* getting smarter! Ha! I mean, yes, Maybe's smart, but when was the last time that you saw a horse keep track of time and distance like I need to do?

I hadn't seen Mom since 9:00 a.m. at the starting line, but I wasn't worried. Sheba and Mom would be far ahead of us, traveling at the ground-covering trot that Sheba and other Arabian horses are famous for. That's why almost everyone who endurance-races rides an Arab.

Maybe was the only mule in the race today. But Maybe suits me well. I'm big, enormous, actually—for a 12-year-old—and Maybe is big too. He carries me easily, as though I were as light as a feather.

A feather! That's one thing you wouldn't compare me to!

I looked down at Maybe's dapple-gray shoulder. He was covered with shiny sweat, but I wasn't worried. In endurance racing you worry if your horse *isn't* sweating. Sweat keeps a horse cool. And Maybe's trot was still springy and strong. He was feeling fine, and so was I.

"This is our big chance," I told the mule. "Today we're finally going to win a trophy!"

Maybe and I were entered in the junior class for children 14 years old and under. As far as I could tell, Maybe and I were ahead of almost all the other kids. And that included all the ones on fancy, expensive Arabians!

I guess I should tell you something about my mule. Mules have a donkey for a father and a horse for a mother, so Maybe looks a bit like both sides of his family. Sheba is Maybe's mother, so he is half Arabian. But he isn't fancy like Sheba. He has a big head and long, floppy ears. His body is thick and blocky, and he has a little stub tail.

But please don't laugh at Maybe. I love him a lot, and I know he loves me back. Maybe has been my mule ever since I was 6 years old. He was born on April 1. In fact, that's how Maybe got his name. On the day Maybe was born my dad woke me up and told me to hurry out to the barn. My dad is famous for teasing, so I wasn't sure if he was playing an April Fool's joke on me or telling me the truth.

"Hurry up, Sarah!" he said. "Mom has something to show you in the barn!"

"Did Sheba have her baby?" I asked.

"Maybe" was all he'd say.

The name stuck, and he's been Maybe to us ever since.

"Just a few more miles," I told Maybe, patting his neck as we trotted along. The finish line shouldn't be far away now, and I didn't want to slow Maybe down.

My dad would be waiting at the 30-mile finish line, along with a vet and a crowd of spectators. Maybe and I could have a big drink of cool water and rest before Mom's race finished farther down the trail. Before any prizes would be awarded, Maybe and the other horses would have to pass a fitness test to determine if they had been ridden properly and weren't lame or exhausted. That didn't worry me, because I could tell Maybe was doing fine.

In a few minutes we came to the base of a long, gradual hill. Maybe stopped before I could pull on his reins. I sighed and slid off slowly, shaking my cramped legs. I knew Maybe would insist that I walk up the hill.

Maybe's smart, you know. He likes me to get off at the big hills. He needs the chance to rest when we climb the slope, and I need the chance to stretch my legs. The only problem is Maybe decides which hills are too big, not me. If I lead him, he'll move quickly. But if he has to carry me, he moves as slow as molasses. You know the expression: as slow as molasses going up a hill in January! That's Maybe. And being slow definitely doesn't win any endurance races.

So I didn't even argue with Maybe. "If you can make it up that hill, I can too," I told the mule. "But first I need a quick drink." I pulled my canteen off the saddle and took a sip of lukewarm water.

Maybe watched me carefully.

"There's no time for a Smartie break," I told Maybe.

Maybe put out one hoof and pawed the air.

"We've got to hurry," I told the mule. "I'll give you some extra Smarties later. Honest."

Maybe sniffed my hands and flipped his big mule ears backward with a groan.

I haven't told you about Maybe's tricks, have I?

Maybe knows lots of them. He can count to 10 by pawing the ground. He can shake hands by putting his leg up in the air. He can nod his head yes and shake his head no.

I've just recently taught Maybe to bow. He doesn't like that trick very much but will do almost anything for a treat. And his favorite treats are Smarties. He also likes soda, but that's too expensive to give him very often. Maybe drinks his bottle of soda in about 10 seconds flat, and then he's begging for another one.

Anyhow, I had a box of Smarties packed in my saddlebags, but I figured it would be best if I waited until the finish line before giving some to Maybe.

I put the canteen back on the saddle and began to lead Maybe up the hill. A worn dirt path wandered back and forth up the slope, and I walked on the rough surface with Maybe following right in my tracks. The hill was the steepest one we'd come to yet, and sometimes I had to learn forward and grab a clump of grass to pull myself along.

I hate being big. I'm the biggest person in my grade, and that includes my teacher. I'm already five feet eight inches tall, and I'm still growing. I guess I'm kind of chunky, too, because all the boys call me fat. FAT! When I look at myself in the mirror I don't know if I agree or not.

My dad says I'm just big-boned. He should know; he's big-boned too. Maybe that's just a polite way of saying we're a bit fat. I wish I looked like my mom, who is small and slim and pretty. In fact, lately I have been praying that God would help me shrink, or at the very least stop me from growing anymore. I guess that sounds kind of dumb. I mean, I know God won't make me shrink. But I hate being so big!

I have to admit that being big can have a few advantages. Not many, but a few. One good thing about being big is that I can beat up the boys who call me fat. I'm just joking. I really haven't beaten anyone up, but I've thought about it.

One real advantage about being big is that I'm very strong for my age. Many 12-year-olds wouldn't be able to climb this hill very fast, but I could keep up with Maybe. And we were moving pretty quickly, because Maybe is the type of mule that can really move—if he wants to, that is.

At the second bend Maybe and I stopped to catch our breath. Until now I'd been too busy concentrating on the million and one things that are involved in endurance racing to pay any attention to the scenery. But the cool, fresh air on the hill path gave me a chance to relax and look around.

God has a really good imagination. In my hurry all I'd really seen was a green blur of trees and grass. But now, when I looked more carefully, I saw details that would have escaped me at other times.

I mean, have you noticed that grass isn't all the same color? New grass is a bright, almost lime-green, color. The longer grass darkens with age, and the ends are tipped with brown. Amid the long grass wildflowers bloomed in clumps. Clusters of brown-eyed Susans nodded softly in the breeze, and several smaller clumps of delicate bluebells dotted the area.

I was surprised at how pretty the hill was. I would have missed all the beauty if I hadn't stopped for a moment to catch my breath. I suppose that's how life is, though. When you're in a rush you don't have time to notice the beautiful things.

Maybe looked at the grass with a horse's eye. In other words, he sighed with relief, and then reached over to take a bite of grass. I bet he thought the hill was beautiful, too—a beautiful salad bar made just for him!

"Don't get too comfortable," I told the mule. "We have a race to finish." I reached over and checked Maybe's pulse and respiration rate. It's important to monitor an endurance horse's vitals, because if they get too high that means they're overworking. Maybe's pulse was a bit fast, but within normal limits, so I figured he was doing OK.

"Are you all right, Maybe?" I asked.

Maybe shook his head no. That's the question I ask when I want Maybe to shake his head. I say, "Are you all right, Maybe?" *Shake, shake,* and then I give him a treat. It's so cute, but today I didn't have time to give him a treat. Maybe gave me a disgusted look when he saw my empty hands. *I don't do tricks for nothing,* he seemed to say.

We started up the incline again. The top of the hill was just in sight when an older boy, riding a pretty brown Arabian horse, scrambled up behind us. I heard the horse before I saw it because his breath was coming in loud, ragged gasps.

That horse is working too hard, I thought. But before I could say anything, the pair leaped forward another few steps until they were right on Maybe's tail. Maybe pinned his ears back at the strange horse.

"Be careful," I said, twisting around to stare at the boy.

The boy glared at me and kicked his horse again. "Out of the way, kid," the fellow yelled.

Maybe bounded forward and swished his tail angrily.

"That jughead better not kick!" the boy growled.

"Maybe doesn't kick," I said tartly. "And you wouldn't have to worry if you weren't crowding us!"

"Move over, fatso!" the boy demanded, "or I'll run over both of you." He began to kick his horse again. The Arab's shoulder bumped into Maybe's haunches, pushing us sideways. Maybe's ears flattened and his lip curled.

"Easy, boy," I whispered. Maybe doesn't go looking for trouble, but I knew he could take care of himself if necessary. But I certainly didn't want to be in the middle of a horse fight, especially on the side of this steep and dangerous hill.

Endurance racing has rules. You aren't supposed to pass until you come to a place where it's safe to do so. And obviously this wasn't a safe place. Suddenly I remembered something that had happened as we drove to the race early this morning. A fast-moving car had pulled out right in front of us as we were driving down the highway. Dad had braked hard to avoid the car.

"Why'd you stop, Dad?" I'd grumbled, worrying about Maybe and Sheba in the trailer behind us. "We had the right-of-way."

"Well, Sarah, you can be dead right and still be dead," he'd said, looking up with a grin.

It seemed to me that this incident on the hill fit in the same category. There was no use in being dead right. So with a final scowl I moved Maybe over, and watched as the boy and brown horse scrambled past us and disappeared out of sight over the top of the hill.

"There's one nice guy," I grumbled. I clicked my tongue to Maybe, and we started back up the hill with a groan. "And look, he gets to ride up the hills!" I complained to Maybe.

Maybe didn't look that impressed.

I really wasn't impressed either. *That horse will never pass the veterinarian check*, I thought. *It's working too hard.*

I guess I was too busy watching the dust of the other rider to notice where my feet were going. Or maybe I'm just a klutz, I don't know. Somehow I caught the toe of my boot on a tree root. It was just a little stumble, but my foot rolled sideways down the hill. My ankle hurt immediately, even before the rest of me hit the ground.

I threw my hands forward, desperately trying to grab something—anything—that would stop my fall. The reins slipped through my fingers. My left shoulder hit the ground with a thud, sending a puff of dust flying. I bounced forward, rolling in an awkward, twisting somersault, a flurry of flying arms and legs, before my face hit the dirt. There was a sharp pain as my glasses smashed against my cheek, and I flipped over and over again, down the bumpy bank. Something scraped against my wrist, and branches ripped at my legs. Dust flew everywhere. There was a sharp pain as my left leg smashed into a rock and my helmet hit something with a solid smack!

The fall took forever, yet it happened so fast.

Finally I slid to a stop.

Tears flooded my eyes immediately. I knew I was hurt. How could anyone fall so hard and not be hurt? But I didn't know how serious it was. I just knew there was a buzzing in my ears and the sky was spinning overhead.

For a moment I forgot all about Maybe. I forgot about the race and winning a ribbon and everything else that had seemed so important a few minutes before. I lay there, my face pressed against the rough bark of a tree, and spit out dust and spruce needles.

2

Back in the Saddle Again

Finally I groaned and propped myself up on one elbow. It was hard to see anything. My glasses were bent against my face and covered with filth. When I touched my cheek, a streak of blood wet my finger. Another cut on my wrist dripped red splotches onto the sleeve of my white shirt. When I shifted my weight, my ankle caught in such a spasm of pain that I sank back onto the dry grass.

"Ooohhhh," I moaned. When I was able to catch my breath, I sat up again, and this time very carefully pulled my leg back under me. "I wonder if it's broken," I said out loud. I wiggled my toes cautiously while rubbing my ankle. In a few minutes the stabbing pain finally settled down to a dull throb.

I'm tough, I told myself. *I can do this.*

I grabbed onto a tree, and struggled to my feet— or should I say my foot, because my left ankle hurt too much to stand on.

"I think it's OK," I muttered hopefully to myself. "Probably just a sprain."

Maybe stood quietly near the top of the hill. It seemed as though he was feeling sorry for me because his big brown eyes were soft and sympathetic.

I swung the sore leg forward and carefully put my weight on it. "Aaaarrghh!" I yelped. "That really hurt!"

I took another small step. The sharp spasms in my ankle shot jolts of pain up my entire leg. My forehead broke out in a sweat.

"This isn't going to work," I told Maybe. "Why don't you come down here and get me?"

Time was passing; I didn't know just how long. I pulled my sleeve back and looked at my watch again. Why, I'd been here only a few minutes! Suddenly I felt terribly alone on the hill. I knew I wasn't in any real danger—other riders would pass me if we stayed here long enough. But I knew they wouldn't want to stop and help me. This was a race, after all. Most likely they'd make sure I was OK, then hurry on to the finish line. Before long my dad and someone on the race committee would come back for Maybe and me.

"We're just about there," I encouraged Maybe. "And think how embarrassing it would be if everyone rides by and stares at us!"

Maybe lowered his head and stood quietly, waiting to see what I was going to do.

"What do you think?" I asked the mule. "Got any bright ideas?"

Maybe shook his head, which made me laugh. Sometimes it almost seemed as though Maybe could talk. Except he couldn't, so he didn't offer me any suggestions.

Finally I decided to do the one smart thing a person can do in a situation like that: I prayed. I know God loves me, and I love Him, too. So praying should always be the first idea that comes to my mind, but to be honest, it isn't. Today, though, it just seemed like the best possible thing to do. So I closed my eyes right there on the hill and said a little desperate prayer.

"Dear Jesus. Hi; it's me, Sarah. I'm having a little trouble right now. How am I supposed to get up this hill? I want to make it to the finish line, but I don't think I can get back on Maybe. I could sure use some help. Thanks a lot. Amen."

Well, I don't know if it was an answer to prayer or not, but as soon as I opened my eyes I had an idea. The first thing I'd need to do was get to the top of the hill. Since I couldn't walk, I'd have to find another way up.

So I got down on my hands and knees and began to crawl up the incline. I was very self-conscious, although I don't know why I was worrying about that. Who was going to see me? There wasn't a soul around except a few birds and a gopher or two. I grunted and groaned as I crawled up the hill like a strange three-legged animal.

I was much slower going up than I had been coming down! My wrist hurt, and my ankle was so sore I kept it tilted up behind me. *My good pants*, I thought ruefully as I ground dirt into the already-soiled knees.

I was huffing and puffing like a freight train long before I got to the top. I almost scared Maybe to death—and he doesn't get scared easily. I suppose I looked like a mule-eating monster as I struggled toward him, flat on my belly, hacking and wheezing, and covered with dirt.

Maybe took one look and let out a loud snort. He spun backward a few steps, then whirled around to stare at me again. His ears were pricked forward, and his eyes were a big as saucers.

"Whoa, boy!" I called quickly. I stopped moving and crouched forward so Maybe could see my face. "Don't run away! Please!"

That would be the last straw. If I panicked Maybe he'd be gone down the path quicker than greased lightning. And I certainly wasn't in any shape to rush after him. So I sat still for a moment, talking quietly to my mule. Maybe narrowed his eyes, almost squinting, as though he was trying to decide who I really was. I could see the wheels turning in his mule head. *Is that REALLY you?* he was thinking, *or is this some kind of new trick?*

"It's me, Maybe," I assured him.

Maybe flicked one ear backward and let out a sigh of relief.

I let out a sigh of my own and slowly crawled the

last few feet up to Maybe. *Thank God, Maybe is a mule,* I thought, flinching as my palm came down on something sharp. A horse wouldn't have taken the time to stop and think. It would just be gone.

When I reached Maybe, I stopped and stroked his velvety muzzle for a moment. Then I crawled past him, heading for the top of the ridge. "Come on, Maybe," I puffed. "We're almost there."

When I got to the crest of the hill, I pulled a couple of cactus thorns out of my knee and then turned to look at Maybe. He was following me, his head held to the side so that he didn't step on the reins trailing beside him.

"Good boy!" I praised Maybe when he stopped near me. I caught hold of his reins with one hand and grabbed the stirrup with the other hand. Getting to my feet was the easy part. Getting on Maybe was a different story.

I had no problem standing on my right foot and putting my sore left foot in the stirrup. But there was no way my left foot could stand the strain and pain of my weight as I tried to swing upward. If I was a skinny little thing it would have worked, but as I've already explained to you, I'm not exactly light.

I hobbled to the other side of Maybe and tried to get on there. But now I had to bear my weight on my left foot and swing the right foot upward. The left foot still couldn't stand alone. The dull throb in my foot was now becoming a sharp, shooting pain that made tears spring to my eyes.

"Ouch, ouch, ouch!" I moaned. "This isn't working!"

I sank down beside Maybe's feet. He looked at me and nuzzled the top of my head.

"I wish you could come down here and get me," I told Maybe with a frown.

Suddenly I stopped. I couldn't get up to Maybe, but he *could* come down to me! Our new trick—bowing for the crowd! If Maybe would bow, the saddle would come down as low as my waist. Then I could just slip my sore left leg over the saddle, and we'd be set!

My book on teaching horse tricks makes it obvious that teaching a horse to bow isn't simple. In fact, it's one of the tricks at the end of the book and it takes weeks to perfect. Bowing starts with one simple step, and then moves to the next. First, you tie a rope around your horse's left front leg. You lift his leg with the rope and give him a treat. Before long, your horse understands that having his foot up in the air is a good thing. Next, you hold a treat (the book suggests carrots) low in front of his chest while his foot is still raised. If the horse bends forward for the treat, you praise him and give him his reward. As the days go by, you insist that the horse goes lower and lower before you give him his Smartie, ah, I mean, his carrot.

After a week you stop lifting the horse's foot and make him lift it himself and lean forward. Before long, a smart horse understands that to get his treat he must lift his front foot and lean forward until his knee touches the ground.

Sounds tricky, doesn't it? Well, it is. Maybe and I had been working on the bow for a week or two. He's smarter than the average horse, smart enough to understand the trick by now, but also smart enough to try and find ways to get out of it!

I struggled to my feet again and fumbled in the saddlebag, looking for the box of Smarties. They were still there!

Maybe's head shot up with the first shake of the Smartie box. The rattle of candies was music to his ears. He raised one foot and began to paw the air.

"We're not counting right now, dummy," I said. "Pay attention."

I slid a Smartie out of the box and held it on my palm. "Maybe, bow down!" I ordered.

Maybe flipped his ears and nodded his head.

"No, don't nod your head. *Bow down!*"

Maybe began to count with his hoof. *One, two, three—*

"Maybe!" I was shrieking now. "Stop being so stupid! We're in a hurry, remember? Bow down."

Maybe shook his head no. Then he looked at the Smartie and sighed. I could almost see the wheels turning in his head. He thought hard for a moment. *I hate bowing. But I guess that's the only way to get this treat.*

Finally Maybe reached one foot forward and bowed his head and shoulders down low. I lowered my hand even further, urging Maybe to get down just a bit more. He obliged by swaying his front half down as low as he could.

When Maybe was at the bottom of his bow I moved into action. As soon as his knee touched the ground, I slipped the Smartie into his mouth with one quick motion, and then bounced my left foot over the saddle. I slid sideways until I was firmly in place, and just in time, too, because Maybe came to his feet with a snort and a jump.

Hey! he seemed to say, *you never used to get on during this trick!*

Maybe pranced sideways for a moment and stomped his feet. He finally got over his pout and allowed me to turn him back down the path.

"Just a few more miles," I promised the mule, "and we'll be done with the race."

Those last few miles were awful. Maybe's fast trot is very rough, and I normally post. (Posting means that I stand up when one of Maybe's front feet comes forward, then sit back down when the other foot comes forward. Posting makes trotting comfortable.) Well, my left foot was too sore to post, so before long my whole backside was aching with every bounce.

"I'll bet I'm bruising my bottom," I complained. "This is worse than being spanked!" Maybe didn't seem to care.

And to make things worse, another horse and rider had caught up with us and were right on our heels, trying to pass. Maybe didn't want them to go by, so he was trotting as fast as his gray mule legs would take him.

"Slow down, Maybe," I begged, yanking on the reins. "I don't care if we win anymore!"

But Maybe did. He packed my big aching body down that path as fast as he could trot, and before long we swept across the 30-mile finish line.

"That was a super finish!" my dad called as he hurried up to us. "I think you're in fourth place!" Then Dad took a better look at me. "What in the world!" he exclaimed. "What happened to you?"

I looked down at myself. My once-white shirt was covered with dust and sweat and blood. My glasses tilted crookedly from my head like a grotesque mosquito antenna. I couldn't see my face, but several twigs were still caught in the ends of my long, dusty hair.

"Were you in a race or a fight?" Dad asked.

"I fell down a hill," I told him, slowly swinging my sore leg over the saddle. "A very big hill. But Maybe picked me up and carried me back."

Dad sighed and shook his head. "Stamp collecting," he said.

"What?" I asked, puzzled.

"I wanted you to take up stamp collecting," Dad continued. "No one gets hurt collecting stamps. Except for the occasional paper cut, I suppose."

"Dad!"

"Or how about playing chess?" Dad suggested. "There's another nice safe sport."

"I don't even know how to play chess!" I laughed. I reached over and rubbed my sore ankle.

"Well, don't come crying to me if you get killed endurance racing," Dad muttered as he took Maybe's reins from me.

I grinned. "I couldn't cry if I was dead, could I?"

"Technicalities, technicalities!" Dad muttered as he led Maybe over to the vet check.

I had a huge grin pasted on my face. My dad's crazy, but I love him.

And Maybe and I? With God's help we had made it back safely again. Now I just had to wait for a while, and see if we had finally won a trophy!

3

Off to the Mountains

Have you ever heard the expression "getting shot in the back"? It means that someone tries to hurt you when you're not looking. Well, that's what Mike and Kevin McConnell were trying to do to me.

Mike and Kevin are brothers. They spend most of their spare time fighting with each other. Kevin, the younger boy, normally sports a bruise or two from Mike's big fists. About the only time they aren't beating each other up they're busy picking on someone else.

This day I was the lucky victim. The McConnells weren't hitting me; they were grunting. Little grunts, then a squeal or two. Sometimes, for a bit of variety, one boy would grunt while the other would call, "Here, pig-pig-pig-pig!" Of course, I was the one they were calling a pig.

I turned around in the seat once and glared at them, but as soon as I looked their way they put on innocent expressions. The moment I faced forward again, though, the oinks and squeals began again.

Shot in the back. And by two creeps who were much dumber than the animal they were imitating. Pigs are very smart, you know. Probably even smarter than mules. And definitely smarter than the McConnell brothers.

"Just ignore them, Sarah," my friend Carley said, leaning forward so I could hear her over the rumble of the school bus. "Those same guys bug me about being too skinny."

"I *hate* being fat," I fumed.

"You're *not* fat," Carley insisted loyally. "You're just big for your age."

"*Fat*," I hissed. "*And* big. I'm a regular giant!"

"I hate it when you talk that way," Carley said. "You're the one who's always telling me that God doesn't make mistakes. Try taking your own advice!"

The school bus door opened with a *swoosh*. I smiled faintly at Carley and hurried down the steps. The bus shifted into gear and roared forward. Carley waved at me, her face pressed up against the window.

Someone else was waving at me. I caught a glimpse of a face at the bus's back window. Then something flew through the air toward me. "Eat that, fatso!" a voice called.

I looked down at a half-eaten apple lying by my feet.

"Creep!" I yelled back. "Come here and say that!"

But it was too late. The bus had already vanished in a cloud of dust. I sighed and picked up the apple. "I didn't want to beat them up anyhow," I muttered.

A loud *whinny—aw-ah-aw* broke my thoughts. Maybe stood in his pasture across the road from me, peering through the wooden fence. I had to smile in spite of myself. Mules have such strange voices, almost as though they can't decide if they're a horse or a donkey! When Maybe brays, he starts off neighing like a horse with a sore throat, and ends with a funny *aw-EE* sound. (Would that make him a hoarse horse? Sorry!)

"No time for snacks today," I called to Maybe. "I've got a lot of packing to do."

Maybe lifted a front foot and waved it in the air, begging me to come and visit.

"I suppose you saw that apple," I said.

Maybe pawed the ground faster.

"It might make you sick," I said. "Boy germs, you know!"

Maybe didn't look the least bit worried about boy germs. I walked over to the fence and set my backpack down on the ground.

"Are you all right, Maybe?" I asked, twisting the apple in half.

Maybe firmly shook his head no.

I gave him a bite of the apple. "Do you like me, Maybe?" I asked again.

This time the mule enthusiastically nodded his head yes.

I gave him another piece. "It's a good thing someone likes me," I muttered, straightening my glasses.

The optometrist had fixed them after my fall last week, but they still didn't seem to fit quite right.

Oh, by the way, I didn't tell you about the endurance race. We placed third! The boy with the tired Arabian that passed us going up that hill was eliminated because his horse didn't pass the veterinarian check. You'll be happy to know that I was polite and didn't even make a face at the kid when I went forward and picked up my award that evening. Maybe and I were awarded a very nice trophy that I have set in a place of honor in my bedroom.

My mom placed first in the open adult 50-mile race. I have to admit it had been a pretty good day for the Ashton family, even if it had taken a while before all my aches and pains went away from my fall down the hill.

Maybe didn't like being ignored. He nodded his head again, this time even wilder. The little tuft of hair between his ears bobbed back and forth. *I like you, I like you,* he seemed to be saying. *Now give me the rest of that apple!*

"Oh, no," I said firmly. "You have to work for it. Just one more trick."

Maybe looked at me with big puppy-dog eyes. Then looked back at the apple.

"Maybe, bow down!" I ordered.

Maybe lifted his head and frowned. (Maybe can frown, you know!) The corners of his lips don't turn down, but his eyes narrow and his ears go back; he looks downright grumpy.

"Maybe, bow down!" I repeated.

Maybe stared at me with mournful eyes and pawed the ground. I put the apple behind my back and stared hard at Maybe. He looked at me, then lowered his head.

"Maybe, bow down!"

Maybe flipped his long ears, and then with a sigh bowed down low. When he was bent over, I reached through the fence and gave him the rest of the apple.

Maybe took it in one big bite and chewed happily. "Good boy!" I praised him, scratching his neck. "And I didn't hop on you this time, did I?"

Maybe finished the apple and sniffed me all over, making sure I didn't have anything else to eat. I wasn't concerned as he snorted and snuffled, touching me with his velvety nose. Maybe doesn't nip, even when he's looking for food.

"Come on, fellow," I finally said, picking up my backpack and starting down the lane toward home. "We have a lot of packing to do today."

My parents and I were going to drive to Nordegg in the evening. We were taking the one-ton truck and the horse trailer and, of course, Sheba and Maybe. My mom's sister, Auntie Teresa, and her husband, Uncle James, had just bought an acreage near Nordegg, which is in the Canadian Rockies. We were going trail riding together. Well, everyone except my dad and Uncle James, who don't like horses.

It was a three-hour drive to Auntie Teresa and Uncle James's house, and if we wanted to get there in time for one of Auntie Teresa's world-famous suppers we'd have to leave soon.

Maybe brayed and bobbed his head when I came to the end of the pasture.

"I've got work to do," I told him.

Maybe hung his head sadly.

"OK," I said. "Just one more scratch."

I could see my mom in front of the barn. She was attempting to wrestle our tack trunk out the barn door so it could be loaded in the back of our truck.

She waved at me and called loudly, "Hurry up, Sarah. I could really use a hand."

"You already have a hand," I yelled back. "In fact, you have two!"

My joke was wasted, because Mom was already out of sight inside the horse trailer.

"The apple's our little secret," I whispered to Maybe, patting him on the shoulder. I really didn't want to tell my mother about the teasing that was happening on the bus. I can take care of myself. I'm tough.

Besides, my mom would just try to cheer me up. She's an optimistic kind of person. I suppose that's a good thing, but it can get tiring after a while. Her favorite saying is "If life gives you lemons, make lemonade." I guess that's supposed to mean that if bad things happen to you, make something good out of them.

Just how am I supposed to make something good out of the McConnell brothers? I thought bitterly. *Or of being big and fat?* I hurried across the yard. I hate being teased.

But then I smiled to myself. *Life didn't give me a lemon today,* I thought, *but it did give me an apple. I guess I should have made applesauce with it!*

Mom and I packed quickly for the horses. We knew the list of horse supplies by heart since we often go on trail rides in the summer. First, there's the riding equipment—our saddles, blankets, breast straps, and bridles. Then there are all the feed supplies—pails, buckets, hay, and grain. We also need our riding helmets and boots and water bottles. So you can see that we really had to hustle to get everything ready.

"It's a good thing you're so strong," Mom panted as we swung the last load of supplies into the truck box. "I couldn't have moved that trunk without you."

"That's me," I said. "Superwoman!"

"All right, Superwoman, I'll catch the horses if you run into the house and tell Dad that we're ready to go. And don't let him forget our suitcases this time, OK?"

"We won't forget them," I laughed. I grabbed my backpack and hurried up to the house.

Dad grumbled as he carried Mom's suitcases down to the truck. "Why do you need two bags, Sarah?" he asked, eyeing my load.

"Because I couldn't fit my curling iron and blow-dryer in with my clothes," I answered honestly.

Dad groaned. "What do you need a curling iron for? I thought this was supposed to be a weekend trail ride for you girls."

"It is," I said. "But I still want to look good."

"I don't think Maybe's going to be worried if your hair isn't perfect," Dad said. But he grinned at me and reached over and yanked the piece of hair that hung in my eyes.

"Set everything in the back," Mom called as we came up to the truck.

Dad looked in the truck box and groaned. "Just where do you think 'everything' is going to fit?" he asked.

"I'm sure you'll manage," Mom chirped from behind the horse trailer. "Where there's a will, there's a way."

That's my mom. I told you she always has something cheerful to say about problems.

I put Maybe's traveling sheet and boots on while Mom worked with Sheba. Our trailer has big windows, and we cover the horses with special sheets or blankets to keep them from getting too dusty. The boots are just padded wraps we use to cover their lower legs so they don't injure themselves in the trailer.

"You look pretty good, boy," I told Maybe, standing back to admire him. Maybe's sheet and boots were bright red, and they looked sharp against his gray coat.

Maybe wasn't that impressed. He stomped his feet

and snorted a bit. He never has liked his traveling boots very much.

"Too bad," I said, scratching his forehead. "It's for your own good."

But if Maybe looked nice, Sheba looked beautiful. Sometimes when I look at Sheba I wish I didn't have a long-eared, funny-looking mule. Maybe could never look like Sheba, who seems to have stepped out of a magazine picture. She could be the perfect fairy princess's horse. Or better yet, an Arabian princess's horse.

Sheba is snow-white now. She used to be gray, like Maybe, but she has become whiter with age. Her mane and tail are long and thick and seem to ripple with every movement. Her elegant dished face and wide forehead and warm brown eyes are picture perfect. People always stop and stare at Sheba when we ride together. They *ooh* and *aah* over her.

No one goes *ooh* when they look at my mule. I guess I'd like to change the way Maybe looks, as well as how I look. I'm too big, and Maybe's too ugly. Well, he's really not ugly, but the way people giggle and stare at him sometimes makes me feel a bit ashamed of him.

"You're a good mule," I told Maybe loyally, kissing him on the muzzle.

Maybe bumped me with his nose. "Cut the mushy stuff," he seemed to say. "Let's get going!" Maybe has traveled enough to know that the sheet and boots mean he's going somewhere.

"I'll get the door," Dad offered, holding it open. Sheba was loaded first.

Maybe stomped his feet and pawed the ground.

"Quit pulling," I told Maybe. I had to keep him from dragging me into the trailer until Mom was finished with Sheba.

"You're such a pig," I frowned. "The grain's not going anywhere."

Maybe loaded himself into the trailer and had started eating before Dad had even shut the trailer door.

"Do you think we forgot anything?" Mom asked, looking around the yard before sliding into her seat.

"The kitchen sink?" Dad suggested.

"Seriously, Doug," Mom said.

"I've never been more serious," Dad insisted. "You have everything else packed."

Dad shifted the truck into gear, and we slowly rumbled down the lane. In a moment we were on the busy highway, heading west to the mountains.

"We should get you a horse of your own," Mom suggested to Dad a few miles down the road.

"No thanks!" Dad answered. "Two hay burners are more than enough."

"Don't you wish you could come riding with us tomorrow?" I asked.

Dad shook his head. "I can see the mountains from the house. Or from the car," he added. "I certainly don't need to be riding out there on some bear bait, checking the scenery."

Mom shot a glance at Dad. "Teresa says they haven't seen a single bear since they moved in," she said.

"Don't tell me that Nordegg doesn't have bears," Dad snorted. "It's famous for bears. And I wouldn't want to meet one while riding a horse in the middle of nowhere."

"They won't give us any problems," Mom said. She smiled at me reassuringly. "Bears just want to live in peace."

"Bears just want to *eat* a piece!" Dad laughed. "But would they prefer horse, or mule? Or are people the best? Let's see . . . Sarah, you'd be soft and tender, with none of that tough skin that a horse has!"

"Dad!" I groaned.

"The only way to be safe is to ride a really fast horse," Dad continued.

"Dad, you know that a bear can outrun any horse."

"That's right," Dad agreed, his grin broadening. "But you don't have to outrun the bear; you just have to outrun the slowest horse!"

Mom laughed.

I smiled faintly, but suddenly the thought of bears wasn't that funny.

Mom seemed to know what I was thinking. "We're in God's hands," she said softly, looking out the window. "We wear our seat belts and try to keep ourselves safe when we drive, but there are some things we have to leave to God. It'll be the same way when we ride tomorrow. We'll do what we can to keep safe, but then we have to leave the rest to God."

Dad nodded his head. "You're right," he said, his voice serious for once. "I don't think you'll be in any real danger."

I wasn't so certain.

4

Bears and Mountain Lions

Dad got lost twice on the way to Auntie Teresa's house. Once when he turned to the right after going through Nordegg, and then again when he insisted on turning right at the same corner after our first trip around the block.

"I'm certain it was this way," Dad said firmly. His grip tightened on the steering wheel.

"We've been this way twice now," Mom said calmly. "And I didn't see a sign saying Range Road 144. Why don't you listen to me and turn left?"

"Who's driving?" Dad demanded. His voice was as tight as his grip on the steering wheel.

Mom shrugged her shoulders. "No one's driving at the moment," she observed. "We're parked along the side of the road."

Dad sighed loudly. "You shouldn't even try to be funny, Becky," he said. "It doesn't suit you."

"Being lost doesn't suit me either," Mom replied.

"Look; here comes a lady pushing a stroller. Let's ask her."

"Don't be ridiculous," Dad groaned. "She isn't going to have any idea where the road is."

Mom ignored him and rolled the truck window down, leaning forward. "Excuse me," she called sweetly. "We seem to be a bit lost. Could you tell me where Range Road 144 is?"

"Are you looking for the riding trails?" the woman asked, glancing at our horse trailer.

"Ah-*hee*-ah," Maybe brayed loudly from the back. *Let me out!* He let his voice trail off pitifully. The baby inside the stroller began to cry in sympathy with Maybe.

"Yes," Mom said, raising her voice to be heard. "We're looking for the riding trails. My sister lives a few miles down the same road."

"You turn left here," the woman said, pointing a tanned finger. "When you come to an intersection, turn left again."

Maybe brayed again and stomped his feet. The sound of his voice in the close trailer made a strange echo that sounded like a cross between a demented hyena and a donkey being eaten alive.

"What have you got in there?" the woman asked. She looked at the horse trailer in fascination.

"A zebra," Dad said, keeping his face perfectly straight.

"A zebra?" the woman asked. Her eyes opened wider than ever.

"Two, actually," Dad continued.

The woman looked from the trailer to Dad, then back again. She didn't even seem to notice her baby's loud wails. "What are you doing with zebras?"

"We're part of a project from the Calgary Zoo," Dad said. "Training zebra to be pack horses in the mountains."

"Doug!" Mom hissed.

Dad smiled at the woman and gallantly tipped his hat. "Well," he said. "We must be off. The giraffe crew is somewhere ahead of us, waiting."

"Thanks for your help," Mom said, gesturing sternly at Dad.

The woman was still staring at us as we rounded the first corner to the left. Maybe gave one last farewell bray, then became quiet.

"I think you were breaking the Ten Commandments," Mom said, shooting a piercing look at Dad.

Dad grinned at us. "Nah," he said. "Don't think so."

"Bearing false witness," Mom said. "That poor woman thought you were telling the truth."

"I doubt it," Dad said. "Besides, I was helping the local economy. People will flock to the riding trails by the dozen if we get word out that zebras and giraffes are being ridden there."

"If they can find the way," Mom said.

"It's simple," Dad said, turning left at the intersection. "Just follow the directions, and you'll get there. Works every time."

"Then why did you get lost?" I asked, leaning forward in my seat.

"I wasn't lost," Dad explained. "I was just taking the scenic route." He suddenly pointed at a sign ahead of us. "There you go!" he shouted triumphantly. "Range Road 144. Right on target!"

"How could you get lost anyway?" I asked Dad. "Didn't you help Aunt Teresa and Uncle James move last month?"

"That was a long time ago," Dad said stiffly. "And it was dark then."

"Isn't 'left' still 'left,' even in the dark?" I asked.

"Never mind," Dad said with a wave of his hand. "All that matters is that we're on the right road now."

"The left road," I corrected. "The right road was our problem."

Dad looked at me and laughed. "OK, kiddo," he said. "You've made your point. Now you better watch yourself. I'll make you walk the last few miles if you're not careful."

"I'd probably get there before you do," I said under my breath.

Dad grinned, and shifted the truck into a higher gear as the truck picked up speed.

Maybe called from the back again, his voice shrill and sad.

"The zebra seems unhappy," Mom said. She looked at Dad and began to giggle.

Dad ignored her and continued driving down

the bumpy gravel road.

🐾 🐾 🐾

Auntie Teresa met us in the driveway. She hugged
Mom, then grabbed me in a big hug. Dad managed to
stay out of her reach by ducking into the garage to visit
with Uncle James, who was tinkering on a vehicle.

"Let me help you unload the horses," Auntie
Teresa offered. "And then we'll eat."

"I'll just help Uncle James with his horsepower!"
Dad called from the garage. The two men laughed
and returned to their poking under the car's hood.

Before long Sheba and Maybe were settled com-
fortably in Auntie Teresa's barn.

"Come on," Auntie Teresa invited. "If we don't eat
soon the food will be cold."

Before long we were all seated around a big
wooden table. Auntie Teresa pulled something out of
the oven, then sat down beside me.

"Would you say grace, Doug?" Uncle James asked,
glancing at my dad.

Dad bowed his head. "Dear Lord," he prayed,
"thank You for bringing us here safely. Please watch
over each one of us, and help us do Your will. Bless
this food, and the hands that prepared it. Amen."

When Dad finished, Auntie Teresa began to pass
bowls of food around the table. No one spoke for a
few minutes, as we were all busy taking big helping of
Auntie Teresa's delicious supper. There were fluffy

mashed potatoes and crispy patties and fresh corn on the cob and an enormous green salad.

When I had finished my first helping and had drunk two glasses of orange juice, I finally brought up the topic that had been on my mind ever since we left home. "Ah, Auntie Teresa, are there any bears around here?" I asked, trying to sound casual.

"I haven't seen any yet," Teresa answered. "Now, could I pass you another cob of corn?"

"I saw some bear scat last week," Uncle James said, sliding the butter my direction.

"Where?" I asked.

"Down by the garden," Uncle James said. "But I don't think he'll give us any problems. We make sure we don't leave any garbage or food out, so the bears won't want to hang around."

I studied my corncob carefully. BEARS! Maybe I would stay home with the men tomorrow. You know, to take up chess or stamp collecting or something safe!

"I hope he won't bother our chickens," Auntie Teresa said with a frown.

"Hopefully, it's a vegetarian bear," Dad chuckled. "He'll just nibble on your lettuce and leave the chickens alone."

"That reminds me of a great joke I just heard," Uncle James said. "It seems this young man had seriously considered being a Christian, but he had decided that God wasn't real. Well, one day he was walking in the woods, and a bear jumped out from the bushes and began to chase him."

I put my fork down and stared at Uncle James.

"Anyhow," Uncle James continued, "the man began to run as fast as he could, but the bear was getting closer and closer. Finally the man fell down on his knees and began to pray. 'Dear God, I know that it's not fair to expect You to help me when I've never believed in You. But if You could just help this bear be a Christian I would really appreciate it.' The man opened his eyes and discovered that the bear wasn't chasing him anymore—he was on his knees beside him, praying. As the man listened he heard the bear say, 'Bless this food of which I am about to partake!'"

Dad and Uncle James laughed loudly. My mom glared at Uncle James, but he didn't notice.

Auntie Teresa seemed to size up the situation, because she looked at me and smiled. "I honestly don't think you need to worry about bears," she said kindly. "I've been riding in the mountains all month, and I haven't seen a single bear."

I smiled faintly.

"Bears aren't your problem, anyhow," Uncle James said, tilting his chair backward. "It's mountain lions that you should worry about."

"Mountain lions?" I squeaked.

"Uh-huh," he nodded. "A cross-country skier was killed by a cougar last winter, near the town of Banff."

"Really?" my dad asked.

"Yep," Uncle James continued. "You know, most

bear attacks are caused when a bear's startled and feels it needs to defend itself. Cougars are different— they attack people to eat them!"

"James!" Auntie Teresa's voice was sharp.

"What?" He looked around the table. "I'm just telling the truth. Mountain lions are dangerous critters. They can kill a man with one bite."

"I don't want to hear another word about it," Auntie Teresa said. "Now, will someone please pass me the salad? Let's quit talking about wildlife."

"I agree, or I may get a little wild myself," Mom said, trying to make a joke of the whole thing.

My mom isn't the funny one in the family. And the thought of bears and cougars was taking all the ha-ha out of me, too.

After supper I slipped out to the barn to visit Maybe. I walked quickly, although it was still light outside and the barn wasn't far from the house.

Cougars and bears, I thought, my heart racing. *Bears and cougars.* I felt like a little kid once again. When I was 6, I had been scared to death of our basement. Anytime Mom sent me downstairs to get a pail of ice cream from the freezer I would run up and down the steps as though the devil himself were out to get me! That's exactly how I felt now. But 12-year-olds have to be a little braver, so I kept myself to a fast walk instead of a dead run.

"DEAD run," I said out loud, laughing weakly. I studied every bush and tree the entire way to the barn.

Luckily, nothing jumped out at me. It was with a sigh of relief that I yanked the heavy barn door open.

And at that very moment something sprang from the dark interior of the barn! It was big and black and hairy, and with a low growl it shot straight out of the barn toward me.

5

Maybe Meets Bo

Whatever that black thing was that sprang straight out of the barn at me had huge white fangs and long deadly claws. I had caught just a quick glimpse, but it was enough. I opened my mouth to let out an earsplitting scream. Nothing came out but a pathetic little wheeze.

Then the bear licked my hand.

It wasn't a bear. It was Auntie Teresa's big black Labrador retriever, Bo, who wasn't very happy about being locked inside the barn when there was perfectly good company to lick.

"Bo!" I gasped. My knees were weak and shaky, but Bo didn't seem to notice as he danced around me, his tail wagging wildly.

I patted Bo on the back a bit harder than necessary. "Stupid dog!" I scolded. "You're lucky I didn't clobber you!"

Bo jumped up and put his big hairy feet on my chest.

"Get down!" I pushed Bo off and found the switch for the light.

Maybe nickered his funny mule call to me.

"Hi there, fellow," I greeted him. When my heart finally quit pounding, I scooped up a bucket of horse cubes.

Bo bounced besides me, wanting more attention.

"Bo!" I scolded. "Keep away from Maybe!"

Bo ignored me and jumped up again.

"Get down," I ordered, giving the lab a push.

"Aw-ah-*aw*," Maybe called. *Don't forget me! Where's my supper?* he asked.

"I'm coming," I said. "Hold your horses!"

I grabbed Bo by his collar with my left hand and swung Maybe's stall door open with the other. "Keep out," I told Bo, wrestling with both him and the bucket.

But Bo didn't listen. With one big lunge the dog broke out of my grasp and danced into Maybe's stall. He bounded toward Maybe, a doggy smile on his big, stupid face. Maybe reacted so quickly that it surprised even me—and I had an idea what would happen!

Maybe's ears flattened against his head, and his lip curled back. He reared up, and as quick as a whip he struck out at Bo with both front hooves.

"No!" I screamed.

But it was too late. One hoof caught Bo on the shoulder and spun the dog around. The dog was thrown against the wall of the stall with a thud. Maybe reared again, towering over the dog. All I could see was Maybe's hooves, sharp and hard as steel, and he wasn't playing. Maybe meant to kill Bo, to crush him against the floor and stomp on him again and again until the dog was nothing but a puddle under his feet.

Maybe could do it. Last year he had found a harmless little garter snake behind his feed bunk. He had crushed that snake until it was nothing but a little ribbon of skin and scales.

Bo backed up a few inches, his face now confused and afraid. But he was trapped in the corner of the stall. He couldn't escape.

"Maybe!" I shrieked.

But Maybe ignored me and lunged toward Bo again, his ears pinned back wickedly.

I threw the pail of cubes at Maybe with all my might. I'm not very athletic but I am strong, and in those close quarters I couldn't miss. The bucket hit Maybe squarely in his chest and caught him off balance. Maybe spun sideways, missing the dog by a few inches. Bo, who was crouched in confusion in the corner of the stall, saw his opportunity and shot out of the barn, yipping loudly.

The yelping soon faded as Bo rushed toward the house. Maybe watched the dog go, and then, with a satisfied shake of his head began to nibble calmly on the cubes that were scattered around his feet.

I immediately burst into tears. Some superwoman I was, crying after the battle was over!

Maybe didn't waste any time on tears. He swished his stubby tail and ate as quickly as he could. Most donkeys naturally seem to hate dogs. And coyotes. In fact, many farmers keep a donkey with their sheep because they're famous for chasing away predators.

"You're not a donkey," I said. "You're a mule, remember? You don't have to attack every dog you see."

Suddenly I had a reassuring thought. "Any bear—or cougar—that wants to tangle with you has something coming, doesn't he, Maybe?" I said thoughtfully. "Perhaps I don't have anything to worry about tomorrow."

I was filling up Maybe's water bucket when the barn door swung open with a thump. I jumped about two feet in the air. I guess my nerves were a bit ragged with all my worries about bears and cougars.

"Hi, there," Auntie Teresa called. "How's Sheba and Maybe?"

"They're good," I said.

"Bo just came up to the house," Auntie Teresa said with a faint smile. "And he has a gash on his shoulder—in the shape of a hoofprint, I think. Do you know what happened?"

"Uh-huh," I said, nodding my head.

"Well?"

I glared at Maybe. He ignored us and took a noisy slurp of water. I twirled a piece of my hair between my fingers and chewed my lip.

Auntie Teresa waited patiently.

"Maybe stomped on Bo," I slowly mumbled.

Auntie Teresa laughed.

"Aren't you mad?" I asked in surprise.

"Bo probably deserved it," Auntie Teresa said. "He still acts like a big puppy, doesn't he?"

I was glad Auntie Teresa hadn't been there to see it all. She probably wouldn't have been laughing if Maybe had turned her big puppy into a throw rug for the cabin floor.

"Maybe hates all dogs," I explained. "Not just Bo."

"Really?"

"Really," I said.

"Well, I suspect that Bo won't bother him anymore," Auntie Teresa said. She leaned on the stall door, studying Maybe. "Your mom says you've taught Maybe some more tricks."

"He can bow now," I said. "I'll show you tomorrow."

"You know, I thought your mom was crazy when she gave you that mule. I wanted her to buy you a pony." Auntie Teresa looked me up and down and smiled. "But I guess she knew what she was doing, because you'd have long since outgrown any pony."

I groaned. "You're telling me!" I wailed. "I'd squash a poor pony flatter than a pancake if I got on one now."

"Your mom also told me that you're worried about being too big," Auntie Teresa continued.

I blushed. Had I said anything to Mom about

being big? I didn't think so, but sometimes moms know more than a kid realizes.

Auntie Teresa sat down on a bale of straw. "Come talk to me," she said. "I know what it's like to be teased about being a giant."

"Who would tease you?" I exclaimed, sinking down beside Auntie Teresa. My aunt is a large woman, but she's still very pretty. I couldn't imagine anyone ever calling her names.

"You'd be surprised," she said. "I was a regular giant when I was your age. I hit my growth spurt before anyone else in my grade, and I towered above all the girls. And all of the boys, as well."

"Really?" I looked at my aunt. "You're not that tall."

"I'm taller than many women," she said. "But not enough to notice now, I guess. When I was a kid all the boys called me 'The Jolly Green Giant.' The girls stared at me in the locker room and made jokes about the size of my chest. I just hated it."

I couldn't resist asking. "Auntie Teresa, you don't seem that big now. What happened—did you shrink?"

"Of course I didn't shrink!" she said with a laugh. "But in junior high the other kids started growing too, and some of them caught up to me. Before long the name-calling stopped. I'll never forget, though, what it was like to be different from the other kids."

"I'm still growing!" I exclaimed. "Look at me."

Auntie Teresa looked at me and smiled. "I see a beautiful young woman," she said.

I snorted. "Yeah, right!"

"I'm serious, Sarah Ashton," Auntie Teresa insisted. "You have such a pretty face—nice clear skin and bright blue eyes and a firm chin."

I smiled slightly. "People don't normally compliment my chin."

"Well, they should," Auntie Teresa retorted.

"But none of that really matters when you're fat!" I complained.

"You're *not* fat," Auntie Teresa said.

"Really," I said. "Well, guess what the boys call me now? Sarah Lee."

Auntie Teresa looked momentarily confused.

"You know, Sarah Lee. It's a company that makes frozen cakes. That's me—a big, fat cheesecake!"

Auntie Teresa sighed. "Honey," she said, "I honestly don't think you're overweight. Today's TV shows and movies portray women as being really skinny, but that's not real life. Real women come in a variety of shapes and sizes."

"Yeah, right." I wasn't convinced.

Auntie Teresa's eyes darted around the barn and came to rest on Maybe. She looked at the mule for a moment and then smiled. "Take Maybe, for example," she said. "Does he look like Sheba?"

I shook my head. "No, but I wish he did."

Auntie Teresa sighed. "Maybe wouldn't be a mule if he looked like Sheba," she said, standing up. She dusted off the seat of her pants. "He'd be a horse, and he'd act like a horse. Enjoy all the neat things that go with riding a mule, including his unique looks!"

I thought about that for a moment.

Auntie Teresa spoke softly. "God loves you, Sarah, because you're His child. Not because you're pretty, or smart, or strong, or hardworking. Yes, you're all of those things, but that isn't why God loves you. He loves you because you're His child. I hope that one day you'll be able to see yourself through God's eyes."

I grunted but didn't say anything.

"Now, come on inside," Auntie Teresa said. "We were going to have worship in a few minutes."

"OK," I told her. "But let me give Sheba a pail of water first."

After the lights were turned out that evening I lay in my sleeping bag and stared at the living room ceiling. The house was quiet, and a stream of moonlight poured in through the nearest window.

I'd like to tell you that my talk with Auntie Teresa had solved all my worries about being big and fat. But it really hadn't. Problems normally don't get solved that quickly, do they?

Being called Sarah Lee and fatso and Miss Piggy hurt. But Auntie Teresa's talk did give me a ray of hope. Perhaps I would be like her, and soon stop growing.

I closed my eyes. *Dear Jesus, please keep us safe tomorrow. I don't want to be chased by a cougar or a bear. And Jesus, please make me a different person—someone who isn't fat. Amen.*

6

Sabbath in the Mountains

Time to get up, Sarah," Mom called.

I groaned and pulled the covers over my head. "I'm exhausted," I said, my voice muffled by the sleeping bag.

"What?" Mom asked.

"I said I'm exhausted," I said, poking my nose out from the covers. "I don't think I slept a wink last night."

"Why not?"

"Didn't you hear the wolves howling?" I asked. "It sounded like they were standing just outside the front room window."

Auntie Teresa laughed. "Coyotes," she said. "It was coyotes that kept you awake. We hear them almost every night."

"That was more than a coyote," I insisted.

"Look, sleepyhead," Mom said, pulling the sleeping bag out of my grip. "If you want to come trail riding you'd better get into gear."

Suddenly I remembered today's plans and sat up like a shot. "When are we leaving?" I asked, fumbling for my glasses.

"Not for an hour or two," Mom said. "We're going to have church here at home before we leave. Then we'll have a big brunch and saddle up."

I groaned. "Do we have to wait that long?"

"There's no rush," Dad called from the kitchen. "The bears will still be there!"

"Douglas Ashton!" Mom shouted.

"Just kidding!" Dad said. "Now hurry up, Sarah. We have things to do."

Auntie Teresa and Uncle James actually had a very interesting church service planned for our family. Uncle James had gone to a lot of work to plan a treasure hunt with Bible verses as clues. The adults followed me as I ran from place to place in the big house, searching for the next clue. When we were all finished, Auntie Teresa read us a story that tied in with the final memory verse.

"Now, before we close with prayer I have a surprise for you all," Uncle James announced when the story was finished. "Today I'm going to play a song for special music."

My dad actually laughed. "You?" he asked. "James, you don't have a musical bone in your body."

Uncle James looked offended. "You haven't heard me yet," he protested. "I'm developing new talents that you aren't aware of."

"I'm sure you'll sound wonderful," my mom said soothingly. "Doug, be quiet."

My dad grinned and leaned back on the couch.

Uncle James left the room and came back in a few minutes with a big case in his hands. We watched with interest as he opened the case and brought out a shiny, gold-colored horn.

"A saxophone?" Mom asked.

"That's right," Uncle James said. "Wait until you hear what I can play."

He fidgeted with the saxophone for a few minutes, then opened a music book to a simple hymn. "Today I'm going to play 'Amazing Grace,'" he said. "Please hold your applause until I'm finished."

Uncle James lifted the saxophone into place and took a deep breath. Then he began to play. At least I think it was playing. I had never heard anything quite like it before. The sax honked and squawked like a goose being run over by a car. Sometimes there would be two or three notes in a row that did sound a bit like "Amazing Grace," but more often the tune was totally lost in squeaks and groans.

My dad's lips were pinched shut so tight that his mouth was pale, but to his credit, he didn't say a thing.

When the song was finally finished, Uncle James set the saxophone down reverently, and with a proud smile turned toward us. "What do you think?" he asked.

Mom cleared her throat.

Auntie Teresa smiled faintly, but didn't say anything.

I glanced at Dad, but he was studying something intently out the window and didn't appear to have heard Uncle James's question.

"Sarah?" Uncle James asked, looking at me. "What did you think?"

"Lovely," I squeaked. "Just lovely, Uncle James."

"Doug?" Uncle James turned to my dad, who was still staring out the living room window.

"H'mmm?"

"Did you enjoy my song?"

"Just beautiful, James," Dad said. "It reminded me of nature."

"How so?"

Dad turned from the window. "It was just like nature," Dad said, beginning to grin. "A coyote howling in pain, perhaps!"

I tried to hold back a giggle.

"Actually," Dad continued, "it was more like a lovesick cow. But definitely something from nature!"

I looked anxiously at Uncle James. His face began to flush pink, then red, and then almost black.

Before I could say anything, Uncle James opened his mouth. But instead of yelling, he began to laugh. He laughed and laughed and laughed. He laughed so long and hard that I thought he was going to choke. And just when he would begin to settle down, he would begin to roar again.

Of course that started us all laughing. Auntie Teresa giggled so hard she fell over the footstool and landed on the floor. Mom had to sit down herself.

Finally Uncle James slid the saxophone back into its case and stood up. "Well," he said, wiping a tear from the corner of his eye, "I'm certainly glad that I could bring such joy to you with my music."

"Some bring joy when they play," Dad said, his face once again serious, "and others bring joy when they quit."

"Let's see you do better, buster," Uncle James said gruffly, giving Dad a playful push.

Auntie Teresa held up her hands. "Enough!" she said, standing up. "Now let's say prayer, and we'll find something to eat. Who wants to help me with brunch?"

"We all will," Dad said. "I had lost my appetite for a while there, but I think it's coming back."

We had an excellent brunch. Auntie Teresa made crepes, and we ate them with mounds of whipped cream and fresh strawberries. There were also scrambled eggs, smothered with onions and melted cheese, and piles of crispy hash browns and thick slabs of buttered toast.

I knew I should be watching how much I ate, but it all tasted so good. I ate two big plates of everything and patted my stomach contentedly when I was finished. "That was delicious," I declared. "But now I'm so stuffed I can hardly move."

"Good plan, Sarah," Dad said. "That way the bear will get filled up when he eats you, and he'll leave the others alone."

"Dad!"

"I have an idea," Dad said, glancing sideways at Uncle James. "Why don't you take James along on your ride?"

"No way!" Uncle James said. "I'm not getting on any horse."

Dad ignored him and continued. "If James went along and played the saxophone, he'd keep you safe. There isn't a wild animal in Canada that would come close enough to listen to that music!"

Mom sighed. "Enough of this," she said. "Let's hit the trail before these men drive us crazy."

"Shouldn't we do the dishes first?" Auntie Teresa asked, looking at the table piled high with dirty plates and bowls.

"We'll take care of the dishes," Uncle James offered. "Won't we, Doug?"

"You bet," Dad agreed. "Anything to keep James's hands busy. I wouldn't want him to start playing the saxophone again."

Mom rolled her eyes. "Come on, Sarah," she said. "It's time to go."

Auntie Teresa owned three horses. "I think I'll ride my baby today," she said. "It will be a good experience for Jesse."

She slipped outside with a halter in hand, and in a few moments led in a horse I hadn't seen before. "This is Jesse," Auntie Teresa said with a smile. "She's 2 years old. Isn't she cute?"

I studied Jesse carefully. She wasn't elegant like Sheba, but she certainly was eye-catching. Auntie Teresa said she was a registered paint, and she did look as though she was painted. Jesse was a bay, which means she had a dark-brown body, and black legs, mane, and tail. Large round white patches covered her chest and her back and one hip, and her black tail had a big streak of white in it.

"I love her color," I said, giving Jesse a horse cube. She nuzzled my hand, begging for another, while Auntie Teresa swung her saddle into place.

"Did you put on Maybe's breast strap?" Mom asked. "And his crupper?"

"Maybe hates the crupper!" I groaned, looking at Maybe. "And Sheba doesn't have to wear one."

"Sheba's not a mule," Mom pointed out.

Most mules have poor shoulders, so when they go downhill, the saddle tends to slide forward. It keeps sliding and sliding, and before long both the saddle and the rider (that's me) can end up sitting on the mule's neck. If you're really unlucky the saddle can go right over the front of the mule's head. That means both the saddle and I would crash on the ground. That didn't sound like much fun, so I rolled my eyes and slipped the leather crupper into place behind the saddle and fastened it around Maybe's tail.

Maybe swished his tail, but didn't make a big fuss. He was too busy sniffing and snuffing at Jesse, who was tied just out of his reach.

"You're such a flirt," I told Maybe, slipping my saddlebag into place. I peeked into the saddlebag, making sure that all the essentials were packed. Yup; there was a water bottle, some mosquito spray, a bottle of suntan lotion, and yes, there at the bottom of the pack was a full box of Smarties. I was careful that they didn't rattle and start Maybe pawing and begging for treats.

"All aboard!" Auntie Teresa called. She led Jesse outside and slipped one foot into the stirrup.

Bo stood behind the barn, watching us anxiously. "Are you coming, Bo?" Auntie Teresa called.

The black dog looked at Auntie Teresa and wagged his tail weakly. Then he looked back at Maybe. His tail slipped between his legs, and he quickly slunk out of sight behind the barn.

"I guess that's a no," Auntie Teresa said.

"Just what happened to Bo?" Mom asked, giving Maybe a disapproving look.

Maybe blinked innocently and tried to sidle a bit closer to Jesse.

"Maybe stepped on Bo," I said, frowning at my mule.

"Stepped on Bo?" Mom asked. "How did that happen?"

"Quickly," I said. "It happened very quickly."

I knew I wasn't fooling Mom. She knew Maybe as well as I did. She knew he didn't like dogs. But I guess she decided that talking about the problem wasn't going to solve anything, because she let out a sigh and clicked to Sheba.

In a few minutes we were heading down the trail to adventure and excitement. I just hoped that we wouldn't have too much excitement.

The first part of our ride was very simple. We rode in single file on a narrow trail that followed the main highway before crossing over the pavement. We then continued another mile or so down the main path. Finally we came to a big sign that announced: "Nordegg Provincial Trail."

"What's with those posts?" I asked, pointing to a set of sharp poles set into the path at close intervals.

"This area has a lot of problems with hunters driving jeeps and such down the paths," Auntie Teresa said. "Those posts solve the problem. Trucks can't drive through the narrow spaces, but bikes and horses and motorcycles can."

"What happens if someone gets hurt?" Mom wondered.

"What do you mean?" I asked.

"How does an ambulance get out there?" Mom asked, looking at Auntie Teresa.

"It doesn't," Auntie Teresa said. "Last fall a hunter rolled his quad over on himself, and the ambulance crew had to haul him out by stretcher. Three miles! Luckily he wasn't in farther, or they'd have really been in trouble."

Mom smiled and tightened the harness on her helmet. My mom can be such a worrywart! I'm a lot braver than she is.

Don't forget the bears, a little voice said in my head. *Or the cougars.* At that moment my dad's jokes didn't seem very funny. I took a deep breath, trying to calm my nerves, and patted Maybe on the shoulder.

Maybe took the chance to grab a bite of grass. He certainly didn't seem very nervous about a ride in the mountains.

Auntie Teresa turned Jesse down the path and through the narrow trail opening. In a few moments the sign and the rest of civilization was out of sight.

7

The Ride Begins

It had been really warm at Auntie Teresa's house, warm enough to make me wish that I could wear shorts when riding. I knew better than that, though. Bare legs against a leather saddle bring up some terrific blisters in a big hurry, so my blue jeans were a necessity.

I sighed with relief as we moved between the towering pine trees. They covered us with sweet-smelling shade, the smell of Christmas trees and warm earth and fresh air.

It had been warm when we left home, but the towering pines soon covered us with their cool shade. The horses' feet swished softly as they marched through the carpet of pine needles. There was an occasional clink as a horseshoe struck rock, and then their feet moved softly through the underbrush again. I listened happily to the sounds of nature around us. Birds chirped from every branch, their shrill trills and cheeps surrounding us with music. My saddle squeaked cozily with each step, and Maybe snorted once.

"It's beautiful," Mom sighed contentedly. "I wish we lived closer."

It was beautiful. The solid green and brown of the trees was broken up by occasional glimpses of unexpected color. I saw brilliant orange mushrooms growing on a fallen tree trunk, and bright-red berries from the wild rose bushes.

We rode in silence for several miles, with Auntie Teresa and Jesse in the lead, and Mom and I following close behind.

"Look!" Auntie Teresa called once, pointing to a branch high above her.

As I watched, two squirrels raced across the branch, and stopped to scold us. "Chit-chit-chit!" they scolded. "Go away and leave us alone!"

I never mentioned the word bear. Or cougar. But I have to admit that my eyes were always darting from side to side, watching for danger. I had just started to relax when I caught movement at the edge of my field of vision. I twirled my head around, trying to catch sight of what had moved there, but now everything was still. "Ah, Auntie Teresa," I began.

I didn't have time to finish. A cloud of feathers whirled up beside me with a loud explosion of fluttering wings. I jumped so high I almost catapulted from Maybe's back.

It was only a flock of ruffled grouse, flying away in

their usual loud manner.

Maybe watched them fly away, then turned his head back to look at me with a puzzled expression. *What's your problem?* he seemed to be asking. *It's just birds!*

I laughed weakly and patted him on the shoulder. *Relax, stupid,* I told myself. *Nothing's going to jump out and eat you. Remember, Maybe can take care of himself, and you can too.*

The path continued upward, climbing steadily. The horses were breathing a bit harder now, and a fine sheen of perspiration wet Maybe's shoulders. But he was cheerful, his ears pricked forward as he climbed. I was glad he hadn't decided that the hill was too steep, or I'd have had to get off and walk.

"Watch the rocks," Auntie Teresa warned, pointing to a particularly rough section of trail straight ahead of her.

I didn't have to worry. Maybe is very agile. Most mules are. They have hooves as hard as steel, and they can travel through conditions that would hurt a horse. That's why they use mules to ride down the Grand Canyon. When you're perched at the edge of a cliff, the last thing you want to be sitting on is a clumsy horse that's about to trip over its own feet!

After a while the path sloped downward. The horses scrambled down the hill, sliding on their haunches, and then stopped by a small stream. Maybe plunged his nose into the water and slurped noisily.

"Could I have a drink too?" I asked, pointing at

the stream. "It looks so clear and clean."

Auntie Teresa shook her head. "It's fine for the animals," she said. "But I've heard of people getting beaver fever when they drink water from these streams."

"Beaver fever?" I asked. "What's that? Do you grow a beaver tail when you drink mountain water?"

Auntie Teresa laughed. "Sometimes you sound just like your dad," she said. "No, beaver fever is caused by a parasite. It can give you stomach cramps and diarrhea."

"Oh." That settled that. I slid my canteen from my saddle and took a big drink. The water was already lukewarm, and I looked enviously at the crystal-clear water that bubbled in front of us.

"You're lucky," I told Maybe.

He swished his tail and began to nibble on the slender grass that grew in clumps near the stream.

"It's really pretty here," I told Auntie Teresa. "It reminds me of a picture."

"Wouldn't this be a wonderful place to have church?" Mom asked thoughtfully.

"Church?" I asked.

Mom nodded her head. "I always feel close to God when I'm in nature," she said.

"I know what you mean," Auntie Teresa agreed. "I think that's why Jesus spent so much time praying in the outdoors."

"I always think of Jesus praying in church," I said hesitantly.

"Oh, no," Mom said quickly. "The Bible talks about Him praying in the mountains and in the wilderness and in the garden."

"So why don't we have church outdoors?" I asked. I closed my eyes and inhaled deeply. The sweet scent of grass drifted through the air, followed by the more pungent scent of pine needles and moist earth.

Auntie Teresa laughed. "This is Alberta, Sarah. I don't think outdoor church would work very well once the snow fell."

"You know what they say," Mom added. "Alberta has four seasons: winter, winter, winter, and almost winter!"

I laughed and scratched Maybe. I tried to imagine the area covered with snow. The little stream would be frozen solid, and deep drifts would bury the trees until only the tops would show.

I wouldn't have to worry about bears if it was winter. Bears hibernate in the snow. I guess I wouldn't be riding here in the winter, either. I don't suppose Maybe would be willing to hike through six feet of snow!

"Let's go a bit farther," Auntie Teresa suggested. "There's a gorgeous meadow ahead where we can get off and have a snack. There'll be more grass there for the horses."

"Maybe always thinks he's hungry," I said, giving the mule a nudge with my legs.

"He's a growing boy," Auntie Teresa said with a smile.

"Yeah," I agreed. "He's growing, all right. But wider, not taller!"

Jesse didn't want to cross the stream. She took a step forward, but as soon as her hooves sank into the bank's soft ground she spun back, splattering mud everywhere.

"Come on, silly," Auntie Teresa urged. "We've been here before."

The little paint didn't seem convinced. She snorted and rolled her eyes and pranced as Auntie Teresa tried to urge her across the stream.

"I can go first," I suggested. "Maybe's crossed lots of water."

Auntie Teresa stroked Jesse's shoulder, trying to calm the young horse. "OK," she finally said. "I don't want to make this water crossing a big issue. I'm certain she'll follow you once you're on the other side."

Maybe strode into the water confidently, his feet making loud sucking sounds as we plodded through. Once we climbed up the bank I turned around and waited as Mom and Sheba made the crossing.

Jesse's movements were more agitated now. "She wants to follow you," Auntie Teresa said, leaning forward on the little mare's neck. "But I don't think she wants to get her feet wet!"

Jesse took one step into the mud. She stopped, blowing loudly through her nostrils, and laid her ears back.

"Watch out!" Mom called.

It was too late. Jesse gathered herself, then sprang forward, trying to jump the creek.

"Whoa!" Auntie Teresa yelled, grabbing for her saddle horn.

The paint's front feet cleared the stream, but her back feet hit the mud. There was a smack as water sprayed across us. Then Jesse was scrambling up the bank and stood trembling beside us.

"Chicken!" Auntie Teresa chuckled, relaxing her hold on the reins. "You'd think you'd never seen water before."

"I saw that water," I said, wiping droplets off my face. "And I felt it, too."

"Sorry 'bout that," Auntie Teresa apologized. "I guess that's what I get for riding a young horse."

"It's not a problem," Mom reassured her. "Now, how much farther do you want to go?"

"The meadow's only a mile or so ahead," Auntie Teresa said. "We'll stop there for lunch, then we'd better head back. It seems to get dark awfully early in the mountains."

I was beginning to relax in spite of myself. It didn't seem possible that anything dangerous could lurk in those beautiful trees on this beautiful day. I guess that's why horror movies always have dark skies and thunder and lightning. It just seemed impossible to believe that anything bad could happen on a lovely day such as this.

And nothing bad did happen. The only living

thing I saw on our way to the meadow was a red-headed woodpecker, tapping in the trees overhead. *I guess I didn't have anything to worry about after all,* I thought with a smile. *This has been a lot of fun!*

8

Maybe Meets Bambi

If you've ever watched the Walt Disney movie *Bambi*, you'll know what the meadow looked like—a lovely green carpet of grass, surrounded by towering trees. I didn't see any deer, but I could easily imagine them grazing on the lush grass.

Maybe could easily imagine himself grazing on the grass, too. In fact, that's what he began to do as soon as we came to a halt.

"Do you think we can let the horses loose while we eat?" Mom asked as she slipped off Sheba's back.

"I don't have any hobbles," Auntie Teresa said. She untied the saddlebag and passed it to Mom.

"We never hobble Maybe and Sheba," Mom said. "They always stay nearby. But I don't know what Jesse will do."

Auntie Teresa shrugged. "I guess we'll find out," she finally said. "Let me take off Jesse's bridle. She can drag the halter rope behind her, but I don't want her stepping on her reins."

Mom took off Sheba's bridle too, and set it on the ground beside her. I decided to leave Maybe's bridle on. Maybe knows to hold his head to the side when he moves, and I wasn't worried that he would step on a rein and hurt his mouth. I opened my saddlebag and took out my water bottle.

We sank down in the grass, and Auntie Teresa pulled out a jug of lemonade. Mom produced a bag of chocolate-chip cookies and an even larger bag of potato chips.

"Pretty healthy meal, hey?" Auntie Teresa laughed. "We've got all the major food groups: potato chips are made from vegetables, and lemonade comes from fruit, and—"

"And Dad says chocolate is a separate food group of its own!" I interrupted with a laugh.

The lemonade was still cold, and I gulped down two glasses of it immediately. Then I ate a handful of cookies, and started munching on the potato chips.

"Sour cream and onion," I laughed. "That's better yet. Onions are vegetables, and cream is a milk product."

Mom rolled her eyes. "You don't fool me," she said. "But I suppose eating unhealthily once in a while won't kill us."

Maybe was stuffing in the food as fast as I was. His stubby tail swung back and forth, swatting at the occasional mosquito that buzzed nearby.

"There aren't very many bugs here, are there?" I

asked, leaning back on one elbow.

"It's not bad now," Auntie Teresa said. "But you don't want to be outside in the dark. I've seen the bugs so thick they look like a cloud. That's why I bring the horses into the barn most evenings."

"Hey, Auntie Teresa," I suddenly said. "Let me show you Maybe's new trick!" I stood up and stretched. "I have a box of Smarties in my saddle bag."

"Don't tell me that mule likes candy too," Auntie Teresa teased. "Why, a person almost needs—"

Auntie Teresa's words caught in her throat. There was a sudden loud crash in the underbrush directly across from us. Jesse's head flew up so hard she almost tripped herself on the lead rope. Maybe and Sheba snorted and took a step backward, their eyes wide.

The crash came again, this time louder, as branches snapped under the weight of something heavy moving in our direction.

"Oh, dear God!" I whispered. I wasn't swearing; honest, I wasn't. It was a prayer, because I had a pretty good idea what was about to happen. I knew that a bear was in the trees, coming straight toward us.

The horses must have been thinking the same thing, because they didn't stop to discuss the situation at all. All three of them shot straight up in the air, and then whirled in different directions, kicking up clods of dirt behind them.

I watched my belongings scatter across the grass from my still-open saddlebag as Maybe galloped away.

The Smartie box flew out and exploded like a colorful bomb, followed by bottles of mosquito spray and suntan lotion.

Then it was quiet. The horses were gone.

The creature in the bushes was quiet for a moment too. I caught a glimpse of something brown and big, and then it slowly disappeared.

I wanted to disappear, too. But where could I go?

It was quiet for five seconds. Then 10. Then we heard it again.

It began as a soft rustle of leaves. Then there was a snap or two as small branches cracked. A strange sound . . . Maybe a grunt. The animal moved closer. Underbrush and tree litter cracked noisily underfoot as the creature pushed its way toward us.

I glanced around wildly. If I had been a horse I'd be miles away already! But I knew I couldn't outrun a bear. Should I climb a tree?

Bears could climb trees too.

Ideas popped into my head with amazing speed, and were discarded just as quickly.

The creature took another step or two in our direction.

"Don't move," Auntie Teresa said. Her voice was surprisingly calm.

I couldn't have moved if my life had depended on it.

"It smells the food," my mom said. Her voice was pinched, scared. I didn't look at her, but I knew what she was thinking, and it scared me more than anything. My mom was thinking bear too.

Dear God, please save us. Please save us. Please save us.

It stepped into the clearing.

It wasn't a bear.

It wasn't a cougar.

It was the biggest bull moose I had ever seen. It took a bite of meadow grass before raising its head to glare at us.

I felt a momentary flood of relief, followed immediately by fear.

This moose wasn't a friendly cartoon animal. He was big and brown and ugly, with narrow pig-eyes that stared at us. An enormous spread of ivory horns towered over his back. He tossed his head as he glared at us, snapping off several small branches with his massive rack. Big horns. Enormous horns.

The moose made a funny sound, a cross between a growl and a cough.

Auntie Teresa and Mom and I stood like statues, staring back at the moose.

A silver thread of spittle swayed from the moose's mouth. He was chewing even as he stared at us, as though he was uncertain whether he should return to eating or take the time to chase these enemies out of his territory.

Auntie Teresa slowly shifted her weight. Without taking her eyes off the moose, she began to cautiously back up. Holding a finger over her lips, she gestured for us to follow.

My legs were as weak as spaghetti. I'd always thought I was tough, that I could take care of myself. I'm big and I'm strong.

But I couldn't have taken care of myself right then. Outrun the moose? I don't think so! I could hardly walk. I guess that's what fear does. This was not the fun-fear that a person gets when riding a roller coaster. This was the big, honest-to-goodness kind of fear that makes your heart pound and your knees turn to jelly.

I did the best I could. I backed up with Mom and Auntie Teresa, trying to keep my knees from knocking together too loudly.

Backward, backward we crept, step by slow step.

The moose blinked his eyes, then calmly reached down to take a large mouthful of grass. He turned his head, following us with his eyes as we slipped farther and farther away from him.

We didn't make a sound. My big feet stepped lightly between each branch and twig. No way was I going to break the trance that Mr. Moose seemed to be in at that moment.

After several minutes of careful back stepping, we were able to slip behind a small clump of bushes. Once we were out of sight we walked faster. Finally Auntie Teresa thought we were far enough, and stopped.

We were all breathing hard, although we hadn't been moving that fast.

"Are we safe?" Mom whispered.

Auntie Teresa nodded her head. "I think so," she said. "He didn't even see us."

"What do you mean!" I gasped. "He was staring straight at us!"

"Moose have very poor eyesight, and we were downwind," Auntie Teresa explained. "I'm sure God was watching over us that time."

"I left Sheba's bridle behind," Mom said.

"And your bridle, too, Auntie Teresa," I remembered. "And all my stuff."

"We'll have to leave it all for now," Auntie Teresa said. "It's not going anywhere. Let's get farther away from the moose before we worry about the horses."

The horses! I'm ashamed to say that I hadn't even thought about Maybe.

We circled the bushes, making sure that we kept something between ourselves and the moose so he couldn't get a clear view of us. I was lost, but Auntie Teresa insisted that we needed to continue to the right if we wanted to reconnect with the main path.

We didn't speak out loud until we were some distance from the meadow.

"That was a close call," Mom said finally. Her fair skin was paler than normal, almost white under her blond hair.

"It certainly was," Auntie Teresa agreed. "A bull moose can be very dangerous in the fall. Rutting season, you know."

"Where do you think the horses are?" I asked, looking down the path.

"I don't know," Auntie Teresa said. "But I imagine they've ran for some distance. I've been told that horses are more afraid of moose than they are of bears."

"What!"

"Honestly," Auntie Teresa said. "Our neighbors' horse herd run through a barbed-wire fence when a moose climbed into their pasture. They spent days trying to track the herd down."

"Maybe won't go far away," I said. I hoped it was true.

"I guess we'll find out," Mom sighed. "We may have a long walk ahead of us."

"But Maybe will be lost," I said.

"They won't get lost," Auntie Teresa assured me. "Jesse knows the way home."

"But Maybe doesn't."

"They'll stay together," Mom said. "I suspect they're already halfway home. Hopefully we'll come across them before too long. I'm not looking forward to walking all the way back."

The walk was much harder than I had expected. My riding boots had a bit of a grip, so I was able to scramble up and down the slippery path, but Auntie Teresa's leather riding boots were treacherous. Several times she slipped down a slope, catching herself only by grabbing at bushes and brambles as she slid by.

"Be careful," Mom kept urging, taking Auntie

Teresa's arm. "I don't want to carry you home."

I laughed in spite of myself. My little mother would never be able to carry Auntie Teresa home. And neither would I.

When we got to the stream, we took our boots off and waded through the ice-cold water. The rocks were covered with slippery moss, and Mom fell once, soaking the back of her jeans. All of us were panting as we headed up the steep bank on the other side of the creek.

"How far do you think we rode today?" Mom asked. She swatted at a mosquito that was circling her head, and pulled her boots back on.

"Oh, I'd guess about 10 miles altogether," Auntie Teresa estimated.

"We have to walk 10 miles?"

"Ten long miles," Auntie Teresa said. "And a lot of it will be downhill."

"Well, I guess that's better than going uphill," I said, wiping sweat off my forehead.

"I doubt it," Auntie Teresa said. "Walking downhill is hard work."

I kept calling for Maybe as we hobbled down one slope and scrambled up the next. "MAY-beee!" I bellowed, but there was no answering *AH-aw*.

I wish I had my box of Smarties, I told myself. *One rattle, and Maybe would appear like magic.*

But the Smarties—and my water bottle—were long gone.

"I'll bet that moose eats them," I grumbled.

Walking downhill was hard work, just as Auntie Teresa had said. Soon both of my knees were aching and stiff. We walked, and we walked, and we walked.

The trees were still beautiful, still green and sweet smelling and fresh. The sun was still warm on my back, and birds still called from the air. But the beauty of the afternoon was gone. I didn't want to be out in nature anymore. I wanted to be home. Preferably soaking in a hot tub, with a glass of ice-cold lemonade in my hand.

"Here, Maybe!" I called again.

After a while I quit calling. My throat was sore and dry, and a blister was developing on the heel of each foot. My hair was damp with sweat when we sank down on a big boulder for a rest.

"I'm thirsty," I whined.

Mom smiled. "So am I," she said. "But we won't die without a drink."

"Could I have one little sip out of the stream?" I asked.

Both women shook their heads.

I didn't argue too hard, because the stream was already long behind us. But the thought of water made my throat feel as dry as cotton.

We rested for a few minutes; then Auntie Teresa stood back up. "We need to keep going," she said, swinging the saddlebag to her other arm.

"Let's rest a bit longer," I begged, rubbing my sore feet.

Mom and Auntie Teresa looked at each other. They didn't say anything.

"What?" I asked, looking from one woman to the other.

Finally Mom spoke. "We can't rest long, Sarah," she said. "Look at the sun."

The pale orb of the sun hung just above the top of the trees.

"It will be setting before long," Auntie Teresa said softly. "We need to keep moving if we want to get home before dark."

I stood up quickly. They were right, of course. I couldn't imagine trying to struggle through these rocks and bushes in the dark. And what about the wild animals? They would come out in the dark. *Bears and cougars,* I thought. *Cougars and bears. That's all we'd need now to finish our already perfectly horrible day.*

"How much farther do we have to go?" I asked as we started back down the narrow path.

"Just a few more miles and we'll be back at the highway," Auntie Teresa encouraged.

"And then we still have to walk a mile or so to get to your place," I groaned.

Auntie Teresa nodded her head and began to walk faster.

The shadows in front of me lengthened, stretching as the sun sank lower. And the miles seemed to stretch in length, too. Every little hill became higher and longer, every little dip became a deep valley.

Rocks that had seemed small when I was on horse-back now became boulders to slide around awkwardly. Gravel that had stood still for the horses slipped under my feet.

We walked as fast as we could, and still the sun sank lower and lower in the sky.

The mosquitoes found us before the darkness did. Mosquitoes and black flies. I'm not sure which were worse. The mosquitoes buzzed in my ears and around my face. The black flies were quieter. They found the warm, sweaty spots and drew blood. In a few minutes the back of my neck and my ankles were clustered with angry, itchy welts.

And the bugs kept coming. They flew in my face and slipped under my clothes. Once I even inhaled a bug and coughed for ages before hacking it up.

The good thing was that it kept me from worrying about bigger animals. It kept me from thinking at all. With every step I thrashed and waved and scratched. It didn't slow the bugs down at all.

Eventually we came to a muddy hollow at the base of some towering spruce trees. Auntie Teresa smiled and knelt down by the puddle. "Come here," she called. She scooped up a handful of mud and began to rub it on her forehead. In a moment she had covered every exposed area of skin with thick brown mud.

I stared at her.

"What are you doing?" Mom asked, wiping a stand of hair from the side of her mouth.

"The early settlers didn't have bug spray, either," Auntie Teresa explained. "So they used mud to keep the bugs away."

"Mud?"

"Just put some on," Auntie Teresa said with a sigh. "You'll see what I mean."

I smashed a couple of mosquitoes, then knelt down by Auntie Teresa. Wrinkling my nose, I scooped up a handful of sticky mud and tentatively began to apply it to my face.

"You need more," Auntie Teresa urged. "You want a nice thick layer."

Mom helped me cover the back of my throbbing neck with the cool mud. "Don't get it in my hair," I said.

Mom smiled faintly. "I wouldn't worry about your hair right now."

"Did you know that more settlers were killed by mosquitoes than by bears?" Auntie Teresa asked. Her voice was almost cheerful now as she helped Mom paint her face with the goop.

"Really?" Mom said.

"Imagine being lost in the woods for a few days," Auntie Teresa said. "You can't sleep, you can't eat—you can't do anything without a cloud of mosquitoes covering every inch of you. There was no way they could escape the bugs. It drove people crazy."

I could understand what she was saying.

"Now," Auntie Teresa said, finally standing up,

"we've got to move on. We should be at the highway before long. Hurry; it's starting to get dark."

"Wait," Mom said. She held up one hand. "You know, I've been thinking. We need to pray."

Auntie Teresa nodded her head vigorously. "You're right," she said.

"I've *been praying!*" I said, trying to keep my face still so the drying mud wouldn't crack and flake off.

"I have too," Mom said, "but I think we should pray *together.*"

"We have a lot to be thankful for," Auntie Teresa said.

"Thankful?" I said sharply.

"Thankful." Auntie Teresa and Mom spoke together.

I guess I lost it then. Forgive me, but it had been an awful day, and the thought of being thankful was more than I could take at that moment.

"Thankful that we're lost in the middle of the woods?" I shrieked. "I'm scared to death that we're going to meet a bear around every corner! And if he doesn't kill me, these horrible mosquitoes will!"

Auntie Teresa and Mom looked at each other, but I didn't pause.

"Thankful that I'm dying of thirst and that my feet hurt?" I howled. "I'm hungry. I'm cold. And Maybe—what about Maybe? Have you forgotten our horses? They're *missing,* you know! *There isn't a single thing to be thankful for!*"

"I'm thankful the moose didn't come after us," Auntie Teresa said quietly.

"I'm thankful it wasn't a bear!" Mom added.

"I'm thankful no one got hurt," Auntie Teresa went on. "If we'd been on the horses they could have spooked and dumped us."

"And I'm thankful that we're together, and that none of us are hurt," Mom said.

I wiggled my feet inside my boots. "My feet hurt," I complained. "And we're lost!"

"Sarah, toughen up," Mom said firmly.

"We're not lost," Auntie Teresa continued. "I know where we are. And don't forget: God knows where we are too."

Mom and Auntie Teresa bowed their heads. I stared at them and then bowed my head too. I was ashamed of myself. I guess today's experiences had shown me a few things. Most important of all, it had shown me that I couldn't trust in myself to get out of big problems. God had already helped me, and I really hadn't taken the time to thank Him for it. And it was obvious that I was going to need some more help before this day was over.

"Jesus," I prayed, "I guess You prayed outside a lot. Well, it's time for me to pray outdoors too. Please help me be brave. Help us get home safely. And take care of Maybe for me. Amen."

9

Lost in the Dark

The darkness slowly closed in around us. It was a darkness unlike anything I had ever seen before. This time there was no flashlight to show the way, no yard light to brighten the dark corners.

Colors and shapes disappeared into the shadows. The path became a ribbon of gray, and the surrounding trees were walls of black. I kept my eyes fixed on Auntie Teresa's coat, which had been a brilliant yellow in the daytime but now was a blob of pale gray.

At first the only sounds I could hear was my heavy breathing and the shuffle of our feet through the thick pine needles. But as the sky darkened, the woods came alive with new sounds. Crickets chirped loudly. Coyotes began to howl in the distance. A light breeze came up and rustled through the leaves in the trees.

An owl hooted overhead. I jumped, and hurried closer to Auntie Teresa. All I wanted was to be home, safe and sound.

Then Auntie Teresa stopped so suddenly that I bumped into her. "Sorry," I whispered. I didn't know why I was whispering, but it seemed appropriate in the dark.

"Listen!" Mom said, holding up her hand.

I listened. At first all I heard was silence. Then I heard a vehicle in the distance.

"We're almost at the highway!" Auntie Teresa said.

"We did it!" I shouted.

The crickets grew silent for a moment, then began to chirp again.

"This way," Auntie Teresa said, beckoning us to the left. "Now keep your eyes open for the sign. Remember, there are posts all across the path, so don't trip on them."

We were just crossing the entrance to the Nordegg trail when I heard a new sound.

It was a low growl.

"Please, God," I whispered, "not another moose!" I couldn't stand another moose.

Then I had another thought. What could be worse than a moose? Well, a bear. That's right. Now my worst nightmare was about to happen right in front of my eyes. (Not that I could see anything in the darkness.) A bear was going to eat me, and I didn't even know which way to run.

I reached forward to pull on Auntie Teresa's coat, but it was too late. The growl erupted into an enormous roar. I glimpsed something dark racing down the path straight toward us. It threw itself into the air and banged into my chest, knocking me to my knees. I let out a horrible scream!

A big wet tongue slobbered across my face, and then the beast bounded away and fell upon Auntie Teresa.

It was Bo!

"You crazy dog!" Auntie Teresa said. Her voice was thick with relief. She whacked the dog's ribs soundly and was rewarded with another slobbery kiss.

I wanted to whack Bo too. With a big stick. That was twice that the crazy dog had attacked me like a deranged grizzly bear. I didn't think my heart could take the stress again.

"Anyone there?" A deep voice called from further down the path.

"Dad!" I hollered. I pulled myself upright.

Bo bounced toward me again, but I smacked him in the chest. "If you ever do that again, dog, I'll put you back in the stall with Maybe," I threatened.

Dad and Uncle James came around the corner, each man holding a bright flashlight.

"Thank God you're OK!" Uncle James exclaimed. "We were worried sick."

"I didn't know how we'd find you," Dad said. "I was just about ready to call the park rangers."

"He tried to phone the rangers," Uncle James said. "I told him his cell phone wouldn't work in the mountains, but he didn't believe me."

"It doesn't hurt to try," Dad said stiffly.

"I know, I know," Uncle James said. "Come on, we're parked straight ahead."

"Off to the right," Dad said, gesturing to a narrow path off to our side.

"Don't be ridiculous!" Uncle James disagreed. "The path doesn't even go anywhere to the right."

"It does too," Dad insisted. "That's the direction we came."

Mom sighed deeply. "Lead the way, James," she said.

"You're going to trust his directions over mine?" Dad asked in amazement.

"And this is from the man who could get lost in his own backyard," Mom said. "Lead on, James!"

Dad frowned but followed close behind us.

"We left the car back by the road," Uncle James explained. He swatted at a cluster of black flies that circled his head. "Come on! You can tell us what happened when we get in the vehicle. Let's hurry," he urged. "These bugs are driving us crazy!"

He shone the flashlight beam on us, and then stopped in amazement, looking at Auntie Teresa's face, and then at mine. His eyebrows disappeared into his hairline. "What's this?" he asked, looking at our filthy faces.

I smiled widely, and a chunk of dried mud fell from my chin. "I'm thankful for mud," I told Uncle James. "At least it's not bugging me!"

Uncle James shook his head.

"Did the horses come home?" Mom asked, taking hold of Dad's arm.

"We found Jesse standing by the barn an hour ago," Dad said. "And we've been trying to track you down ever since."

"What about Maybe and Sheba?" I asked.

Dad shook his head. "We haven't seen them," he said. "I thought they would be with you."

In a moment we were at the car. Dad opened the door, and we all slipped inside.

"Did you get bucked off?" Dad asked, turning around to look at us.

Mom shook her head and quickly explained the situation.

"A moose!" Uncle James exclaimed. "You're lucky he didn't charge you. They can be wicked in the fall."

"I know," Auntie Teresa said quietly.

"Dad, Uncle James," I said, "we need to use your flashlights. We have to go back for Maybe and Sheba."

"We won't find them in the dark," Auntie Teresa said.

"What should we do?" Dad asked.

Auntie Teresa was quiet for a moment. "I'll tell you what my biggest worry has been," she said in a soft voice. "I've been afraid that the horses will run across the highway and be struck by a car. You didn't see anything lying in the ditch on the way over, did you?"

Both men shook their heads.

"I don't think there is much we can do in the dark," Auntie Teresa said reluctantly. "Let's go home and see if they're there now."

A very anxious-looking Jesse stood alone in one of the barn stalls. Her halter was still on, but the rope was tattered and torn. A deep gouge marked Auntie Teresa's saddle, but the horse herself seemed unhurt.

Auntie Teresa slipped the saddle off and shook pine needles out of the saddle blanket.

"Where's Maybe?" I asked the little mare.

Jesse sighed, and lowered her head.

"Let's put a pile of hay in front of the barn," Mom finally suggested. "That way Maybe and Sheba will have something to eat if they find their way back here tonight."

"*If* they find their way back?"

"*When* they find their way back," Mom corrected herself firmly.

"Can't we go looking for them?" I asked.

Mom shook her head. "Sarah, how much could we see when we were in the forest tonight? Would we be able to find the horses?"

"We could if we had the flashlights," I said stubbornly.

"No, we couldn't," Mom disagreed. "The forest is too big."

"So what are we supposed to do?" I asked.

"We'll pray about it," Auntie Teresa said. "And then we'll go looking first thing in the morning."

"I'll get up in the night and check to see if they found their way back," my dad offered.

I glanced at him. "You don't even like horses."

"But I like you and Mom," Dad said. "And that's what counts."

As soon as we got home I drank two full glasses of water. Then I ran water in the bathtub, right to the top, and, slipping off my clothes, I popped over the edge.

"Ahhh! This is lovely!" I breathed. I hadn't realized how cold I'd been until I felt the hot water tingling my cold, aching feet. The blisters on my heels had opened, and they stung in the bathwater momentarily. I sank down so the bubbles covered everything from my chin down and sighed.

What a day!

I was OK. The pain in my heels was nothing. But Maybe . . . He could be anywhere. The Nordegg path covered mile after mile of trails, some leading into the back country. I wasn't sure when hunting season began, but I hoped it wasn't soon. Hunters were welcome to Mr. Moose, but not Maybe.

My stomach began to lurch and churn. I must have drunk too much water, I guessed, and worry on top of it all probably wasn't helping things.

I closed my eyes, and splashed warm water on my face, washing off the last of the dried mud. My imagination took over as soon as I closed my eyes. I saw Maybe in the woods, kicking and struggling with a grizzly bear. I saw him bolting across the highway, straight into the blazing headlights of a truck. I saw him alone and frightened and hurt. I quickly opened my eyes.

Oh, my stomach was really hurting now. I almost felt as though I was going to be ill.

Stop worrying, silly, I told myself. *Remember what Mom said: God will take care of Maybe.* I wondered how God could actually find the time to worry about my mule. He had to be busy with all the world's problems—war, earthquakes, and other disasters. Could God—would God—actually help Maybe?

Then I thought of my dad. My father didn't like horses, but he liked me, and that was enough. I knew without doubt that God loved me, too. I guess that makes my problems His problems. "Please take care of Maybe," I whispered. "I can't help him, but You can."

I fell into a restless sleep on the living room couch. In my dreams a moose was chasing me through the forest. It came closer and closer . . . It knocked me down . . . It gouged me in the stomach with its cruel horns . . . It stabbed me again and again!

My stomach was hurting. I woke up from the dream to discover that the pain was all too real. "I'm going to puke!" I groaned. I sat up in the dark room quickly, and the ceiling spun around me. I struggled to my feet, groping for the floor lamp. I had to get to the bathroom—and quick—or I was going to throw up all over Auntie Teresa's rug!

I got to the bathroom just in time. I vomited everything I had drunk or eaten that evening. And still I kept heaving, even when my stomach was so empty that it clung to itself like a ball of wadded up Saran wrap.

I must have started crying, because Mom came down to the bathroom, her robe wrapped around her. "What's wrong, Sarah?" she asked.

"I'm sick," I said. My stomach was hurting even worse now, and although I was burning up, I began to shiver.

"Did you throw up?" she asked. She looked into the toilet and wrinkled her nose.

"I feel horrible," I said.

Mom looked at me, then back at the toilet. "Sarah," she said slowly, "did you drink water when we were horse riding?"

I nodded my head.

"From the stream?" she asked.

"No!" I exclaimed weakly. "Just from my water bottle."

"Are you sure?"

"Yes, I'm sure," I said. "I wouldn't lie."

"I know, I know," Mom said. She felt my forehead. "I believe you. But I just got to thinking about beaver fever, and I wondered . . ." Her voice trailed off.

"I didn't drink any of that water," I said. "I must have the flu."

"Yes, you're sick," Mom said. "Here, let me wash your face, and then you can go back to the couch."

"I'm going to throw up again," I said.

"I'll bring you a pail," Mom said. "Come on; back to bed."

It was a horrible night. I dozed off for brief periods

of time, but mostly I lay on the couch with my knees tucked up to my chest, trying to ease the pain in my abdomen. I couldn't remember ever having been so sick before.

What a terrible day!

And what about Maybe? How was I going to search for him tomorrow?

I woke up a few hours later to the sound of pots and pans banging together in the kitchen. I wasn't nauseated anymore, but my stomach still ached and my throat was sore. I could taste my own breath, and it wasn't good.

"Morning, sleepyhead," Dad greeted me, poking his head around the corner. "Are you feeling better?"

I shrugged my shoulders. "A bit," I said. "Did Maybe come back?"

He shook his head.

"What about Sheba?" I asked, sinking back into the couch.

"Nope," he said. "Your mom and Auntie Teresa are going out to look for them right away."

"I want to go too," I insisted.

"Not now," Mom said from the doorway. "You're in no condition to ride a horse."

"I am too," I objected, sitting up quickly. The walls tilted and turned, but at least the ceiling didn't spin overhead this time.

"No, you're not," Dad said. "You can help me make posters."

"Posters?"

"I'm going to scan some pictures of Maybe and Sheba in Uncle James's computer and make some posters. Someone is sure to find the horses," Dad explained. "Now they'll know how to contact us." He stood up and began to walk toward the kitchen. Suddenly Dad stopped and pointed out the big living room window. "Look!" he called.

Everyone raced to the window. I scrambled to my feet and staggered over beside them.

There, hobbling down the driveway, was a horse, a gray horse! It was Maybe! Then I looked more carefully. No, that wasn't Maybe's big head and floppy ears. It was Sheba. I looked around the yard, expecting to see Maybe behind his mother. But he didn't appear.

"Why's she limping?" Dad asked.

Mom was already outside and halfway to the barn.

I pulled on my blue jeans and a faded sweatshirt, and dragged myself outside. I squinted in the bright morning sunshine.

"Is she OK?" I asked.

Mom had her arms wrapped around Sheba's neck. "She's fine," Mom said. "Just fine. It's only her shoe."

"What's wrong with her?" Dad asked from behind me.

I wobbled a bit, and Dad reached over and propped me straight with his big arms.

"Nothing serious," Mom said. Her voice was happy. "She's pulled a horseshoe loose, and some of the nails are pressing against the sole of her hoof."

"That's all?" Auntie Teresa asked, bending over and looking at Sheba's foot.

"That's all," Mom said. "Come on, girl. Let's get that miserable shoe off your foot. And I bet you'd like some breakfast."

Mom turned to lead Sheba forward, and then stopped. She looked at my face, which must have been stricken. "Don't worry, Sarah," she said. "I'm sure Maybe will be here soon. Everything's going to be OK."

I turned and hurried back to the house. First, I was going to puke. Then I was going to have a long, hard cry.

10

Searching for Maybe

I lay on the couch, my eyes closed tightly. The sensation of motion had returned, and I opened my eyes to be certain I really wasn't moving.

"Maybe's the smart one," I said to no one in particular. "Why hasn't he come home yet?"

"He'll be back," Mom promised.

"I read a story about two horses lost in the mountains once," I said. "Some hunters lost their horses. They found one the next day. The other didn't come back for weeks."

"Well, at least they finally found him," Dad said.

"Not until he was badly hurt," I said. "His saddle slipped sideways, and his breast strap cut into his shoulder. Every time he took a step the strap cut deeper into his flesh."

"Maybe will be fine," Mom repeated firmly. But her voice sounded a bit tighter to me.

"Oh, sure he will," I said. "Except he's got his saddle on, too. What if it's slipping sideways and cutting into him? Or what if his bridle is hooked on a bush, and he can't move?"

"Sarah!"

"We have to find him, Mom," I cried. "And soon—before the bears do."

Mom turned and stared at Dad. "You see? We need your help. Please, Doug," my mom begged. "We really need your help."

"No," my dad said. He shook his head determinedly.

"Please?" Mom repeated.

Dad beckoned to me. "Come here and give me a kiss, Sarah," he called.

"Why?" I asked, sitting up on the couch.

"I'd rather be sick with the stomach flu than ride a horse through the mountains," Dad said. He seemed serious.

"I'll come with you, Mom," I said.

"You're sick," Mom said. "Your job is to baby-sit the phone."

"I've done my share," Dad insisted. "I hung posters by the trail entrance, and several in town, and I've phoned the park ranger's office. Isn't that enough?"

"No," Mom said stubbornly. "We need to cover as much territory as possible today. And I don't want to be caught in the dark again."

"What about Uncle James?" I asked.

"Didn't I tell you?" Dad said. "He's sick too."

"Dad's right," Mom said. "Uncle James has been

in the bathroom all morning, sitting on the toilet with a pail in his hands."

I giggled weakly.

"Teresa has been gone for almost an hour now," Mom said. "She took Jesse down the path where we rode yesterday."

"Goody for her," Dad said.

"I would like to head west," Mom said, "and look for Maybe there."

"I don't know how to ride a horse," Dad pointed out. "I'd be more hindrance than help."

"I want someone to come with me," Mom insisted.

"Why?"

Mom blushed. "Well," she said slowly. "I'm a bit chicken, if you want to know the truth."

"Chicken?" I asked blankly.

"I wouldn't want to meet a moose," Mom said slowly. "Or a bear, or anything. Especially if I didn't have someone with me."

"So you want the bear to eat me instead of you," Dad said carefully. He still wasn't laughing.

"I just want a little bit of moral support." Mom frowned. "Is that asking too much?"

Dad sighed.

Mom put her hands on her hips and waited for a moment. "Well, is it?" she repeated.

"OK," Dad said. "I surrender. I'll help you look for Maybe. But I better not have to do anything except hang on. And point you in the right direction, of course."

"Fine," Mom said. Her voice softened. "I really appreciate it, honey. And I want you to know that you fit John Wayne's definition of courage."

"And what would that be?" Dad asked, a faint smile edging his face.

"He said that courage is being scared to death—and saddling up anyway!"

Dad ran his fingers through his hair. "All right, little lady," he drawled in his deepest John Wayne voice. "Let's hit the dusty trail."

They left about a half hour later. I watched them ride past on Auntie Teresa's horses. Mom waved, but Dad didn't take his eyes off the path in front of him. I thought, *He's going to have a sore hand before long, holding onto the saddle horn that tight!*

I looked at the clock. It was only 10:30 in the morning. A lot had happened in the past few hours. I wondered what I should do . . . I could go outside and call for Maybe. He'd come if he could hear me. Or I could phone the park rangers and see if they'd found my mule.

It took me a few minutes to find the phone book and dial the number. "This is the Nordegg Provincial Park Office," a voice chanted.

"I've lost my mule," I said. "And I wonder if anyone—"

"Office hours are from 12:00 noon till 5:00 p.m. on weekends, and from 8:00 a.m. to 8:00 p.m. on weekdays," the voice continued. "Please leave a message, and we'll get back to you as soon as possible. Thank you!"

A lousy recording! I was trying to find my mule, and all I could do was talk to a recording. "God, you've got to help me find Maybe," I groaned, hanging up with a bang. It didn't look like anyone else was going to be of any help.

I thought about my parents riding through the trees. Dad was probably already lost and traveling in big circles through the underbrush.

"I'll just rest a few minutes," I said out loud. "Then I'll go outside and call for Maybe."

I must have fallen asleep, because it was almost 11:30 when Uncle James woke me up. "Sarah," he croaked, "do you have any Gravol?"

"Gravel?" I asked, sitting up on the couch. I wasn't dizzy anymore but my stomach still ached dully.

"Gravol," he repeated. "It's medication for nausea."

I shook my head. "No, Uncle James, I don't have any medicine with me."

He groaned loudly. "I can't stand it anymore," he said. "I've got to do something."

"Mom and Dad should be back before long," I said. "They'll help you."

He thought for a moment. "I'm going into town," he finally said. "If the convenience store doesn't carry Gravol, I'll knock on every door until I find someone who does."

"Do you want me to come with you?" I asked,

eyeing Uncle James. He looked terrible. Even his hair was wilted and sick-looking.

"No," he answered. "I'll be OK. You could use some more rest."

I lay back down on the couch obediently.

"I shouldn't be gone for more than an hour or so," Uncle James said, fishing in the closet for his coat. "Let's see . . . Twenty minutes to town and 20 minutes back. Or I may be longer; it's hard to say."

"I don't mind staying home alone," I assured him. "I want to hang around in case someone phones. I'm hoping someone will see the posters that Dad hung up about Maybe."

"Oh, Sarah!" Uncle James said. "I'm sorry. Auntie Teresa told me he didn't come back yet. But don't worry; I'm sure he's OK."

"Uncle James," I suddenly blurted, "why does God let bad things happen? Maybe didn't do anything wrong."

Uncle James sighed and sank down beside me on the couch. "That's a good question, Sarah," he said slowly. "And I'm not sure that I have all the answers. I'm not sure that anyone has all the answers to evil in this world."

"Someone once told me that God lets bad things happen to us so we'll learn from our problems," I said. "Do you think that's true?"

Uncle James thought for a moment. "I think that can be true," he said. "But I don't think that's the whole answer."

"So what's the answer?"

"Sarah, many years ago my parents were in a terrible vehicle accident," Uncle James said. "They were both killed."

"I didn't know that," I said in surprise.

"It happened before I was married to Auntie Teresa," Uncle James continued. "My mom and dad were good people—good Christians who had tried to serve Jesus all their lives. They didn't do anything to cause the accident, and neither did the other driver. His vehicle hit a sheet of ice, and he slid into my folks. All three died at the scene of the accident."

"That's terrible!"

"Yes, it is." Uncle James's face was sad. "I still miss them, you know."

I didn't say anything, because I didn't know what to say.

"Anyhow, that accident really made me think about God," Uncle James said softly. "Why does He allow bad things to happen? Why doesn't He help everyone who prays for help?"

"That's what I want to know," I said.

"I'm not a pastor," Uncle James continued. "But I'll tell you what I believe. I believe that bad things happen for different reasons. Yes, sometimes God allows tragedy because He knows the future and knows that what looks horrible for us is really the best thing."

"Like what?"

"Think how Jesus' disciples were persecuted. Their

suffering helped bring God's Word to people all around the world. So sometimes good can come out of bad."

"I guess so," I agreed slowly. "But I don't see how anything good could come out of your parents being killed."

"I can't either," James said. "But maybe God can. That's not the only reason bad things happen in this world. I believe that sometimes bad things happen because we make bad choices that harm us. For instance, the person who drinks and drives. If they have an accident, it isn't because God caused the accident but because God gives them the free choice to make good or poor decisions."

I nodded my head. "That makes sense," I said.

"And don't forget Satan," Uncle James continued. "He wants to hurt us all. Sometimes he does it by making us rich and proud, so that we grow away from God. Sometimes he does it by harming us and hoping that we'll blame God for our pain."

"Do you think God can answer prayers?" I asked.

Uncle James smiled weakly. "I know He can," he said. "He always answers our prayers. And He answers them in the very best way. Sometimes that means that He says yes, and sometimes it means that He says no."

"Do you think it's OK for me to pray about Maybe?"

Uncle James stood up. "Of course it is, Sarah," he said. "God cares about Maybe. But don't forget: when you pray, you need to ask God to do what He thinks is best, not what you think is best."

I sighed. "I'll try, Uncle James, but it's hard."

"I know it is," he said. "Don't forget that real life isn't like a storybook—prayer, with magical endings. Sometimes we pray and never see our prayer answered. We need to trust God with that, too."

"I know what you mean," I said. I thought about some of my prayers this year. They seemed almost silly now. I mean, I'd been praying that God would make me small, like my friend Carley. Perhaps God really did know what was best for me. But sometimes it was hard to really trust Him.

"Now would it be OK if I drive into town? I feel awful, and I'd like to find something to help me," Uncle James said with a groan. Each freckle stood out on his pale face.

"Oh, I'm sorry, Uncle James," I said. "Thanks for taking the time to talk to me."

"My pleasure," he said. "Now, where's that bucket? I don't want to go anywhere without it."

Uncle James had barely driven out of the yard when the phone rang. I scrambled over the couch and found the portable phone buried under a stack of papers on the counter.

"Hello," I said.

"Hello, 'ello, 'ello!" A loud voice boomed into the phone. "Would this be the wee lassie who's lost 'er donkey in the backcountry?"

"Ah—yes, this is her—I mean, it's me. I lost my mule yesterday."

"Aye," the voice continued. "Excellent then. One of ma men 'ere at the park office has been notified that there's a donkey down by the highway. I'm thinkin' that it's yours an' all."

"Someone found Maybe?" I burst out excitedly.

"Well now, I wonna say they found ya donkey. But they heard sommat makin' a big noise when they were walkin' along the highway there. Loud noise, they said, back in the bushes a'ways. You know, 'hee-haw' an' all. I figure it must belong to the donkey ya lost."

"Where did they hear the noise?" I asked, grabbing a piece of paper.

"Why, not far from where ya live, lassie," the man laughed. "Jus' a hop an' a skip down the highway there. 'Bout a mile or so, I'd say. Straight north, an' ya can't miss 'im."

"That's wonderful!" I was already reaching for my blue jeans.

"Good luck, lassie," the man called. "I'm off then."

The phone hung up before I could even say goodbye.

"Hee-haw an' all." That had to be Maybe! But why would he be standing in the trees near the highway? Wouldn't he just come on home? Perhaps his reins were tangled up. Or he was hurt and couldn't walk.

I looked at the clock. Uncle James wouldn't be back for at least an hour. And he wouldn't be much help anyhow. He was sick. Even when he was well he didn't ride any better than Dad. I didn't know when to expect Mom and Dad and Auntie Teresa back. They could be gone until dark. No; if anyone was going to check along the highway for Maybe, it was going to have to be me.

I slipped a heavy sweater over my T-shirt and carefully pulled my socks over my sore heels. I was hardly dizzy at all now, and although my stomach was grumbling and groaning, I didn't feel like throwing up. How hard could it be? Just a short ride out along the highway.

I had to pause when I got to the barn. I hadn't thought very far down the line, and it wasn't until I got into the barn that the first obstacle presented itself.

Was Sheba sound enough to ride? She was the only horse left on the place. Mom had pulled off Sheba's loose shoe, which meant she would now be shod on three hooves and barefoot on the fourth. I slipped the halter on Sheba and lead her down the barn's alleyway.

Was she limping? No, she set each foot down easily.

"We'll have to avoid the rocks," I told Sheba. "But I think you'll be OK."

The next problem came when I went to tack Sheba up. Mom's saddle was gone. On Auntie Teresa's horse, I supposed. My saddle was gone, too, and I had to think for a moment, until I realized that it was still on Maybe, wherever he was.

I suddenly pictured Maybe with the saddle hanging sideways from his back. He was trembling, the leather breast straps pulled snug around his neck. There was a trickle of blood from an open sore, and behind him in the trees a mountain lion lurked.

"Stop it!" I scolded myself, opening my eyes. I had things to do. I could worry about Maybe later. Now I had to find tack for Sheba.

Sheba's bridle lay out in the meadow somewhere. Hopefully Mr. Moose hadn't bothered it.

There was one saddle left in the tack room. It was Auntie Teresa's tiny English saddle. I had never ridden English before, but how difficult could it be?

"Very difficult," a tiny voice said in the back of my head.

I ignored the voice and swung the saddle up onto Sheba's back. It took a few minutes of adjusting to do the cinch up tightly, and then I had to pull the stirrup straps down and lengthen them to fit my long legs.

"Now a bridle," I muttered, casting my eyes around the tack room. Sheba's bridle was nowhere in sight. It still lay on the meadow floor, too, I imagined. Unless the moose had come along and eaten it.

A matching English bridle with shiny snaffle bit hung just above the place the saddle had hung. That would do, I imagined. Sheba was used to a snaffle. This took a little longer to adjust. Sheba was amazingly patient while I fiddled with straps and buckles until if finally hung properly on her head.

"I hope this works," I said, stepping back to admire my job.

I strapped my riding helmet on, sprayed myself with mosquito spray, and picked up an extra rope to carry with me. I didn't know what to expect when I found Maybe. It was quite possible that his bridle had been destroyed or lost. If so, the rope would come in handy.

I led Sheba out of the barn and pulled the door shut behind me. I hesitated before mounting. My cheeks felt hot and flushed. I wasn't sure if my flu was causing that, or nerves. I was dreading the ride alone in the mountains. Plus, I wasn't that familiar with Sheba, and that frightened me too.

I wouldn't allow myself to think about bears. Meeting the moose yesterday had been enough for me. And I had survived that. *I won't worry anymore,* I determined. *I'll leave the worrying to God.*

I bowed my head quickly. "Dear God, it's Sarah again. I hope You aren't getting tired of hearing from me. Please help me find Maybe. Please watch over him for me. And keep all of us safe. Thanks a lot for caring about me and for hearing my prayer. Amen."

11

Caught!

I was perched on the narrow English saddle, scared spitless, and trying to keep Sheba from knowing that. This ride was not exactly a dream come true. It was more like a nightmare!

I kept the reins a bit tighter than necessary as we turned off the driveway and started down the path that followed the highway. I had ridden Sheba only once or twice before, and I didn't trust her very much. The English saddle felt strange. The stirrup leathers swung back and forth like pendulums, and there was no saddle horn to grab onto if the going got tough.

"If the going gets tough, I'll just get tough, too," I said out loud.

Only a few short days ago I would have believed what I said, but now I knew the real truth: I was the sort of person whose knees knocked during danger! Who was I kidding with my big talk? Not myself. Not Sheba. And certainly not God!

An added problem was my lack of knowledge of the area. The man at the park office (the one with the funny accent) had said I needed to go north. I still could hear his peculiar voice: "'Bout a mile or so, I'd say, straight north an' ya can't miss 'im."

I hoped he was right.

North. I thought for a moment. If the main trail went west into the mountains, then north would have to be to my right. That would make sense, because the highway ambled in a northward direction, at least most of the time. I figured that I would ride as far as the Nordegg trail sign, and then decide what to do. Hopefully, there was another path that followed along beside the highway.

In about 10 minutes Sheba and I were at the sign. Sheba was behaving very well, and I was beginning to trust her more. She had even remained calm when a motorcycle roared past us with only a few feet to spare.

"Good girl," I told Sheba, patting her on the shoulder. "And your hoof isn't hurting you, is it?"

I pulled her to a halt and looked around. The main path was straight ahead. Sheba bobbed her head, wanting to go that direction, but I kept her still. We had ridden this way yesterday. Was it only yesterday? It seemed like a million things had happened since the last time I had ridden through those posts.

I tried to visualize that ride. Was there another path going north? I couldn't see any trail wide enough for a horse and rider to travel on. I swung Sheba around in a big circle, looking for an alternate route. No luck. Sheba wasn't pleased with my efforts, but obeyed me sullenly.

I was beginning to get discouraged. It hadn't seemed that difficult when I was at home, parked on the nice safe couch. "Straight north," the man had said. But how did I go north? And what if I had my dad's sense of direction? I would be doomed!

Sheba took a few steps toward the main path, and I hesitated. Finally I loosened the reins, allowing Sheba to head that direction. In a moment we were through the narrow opening.

"Now what?" I asked the horse.

We had only gone a short distance when I noticed a second trail breaking away from the one we had ridden on yesterday. It was to the right—going north! Yes! Now we were on the right track—literally, I hoped! I swung Sheba down the path. Sheba seemed pleased with my decision, and quickened her pace.

The trail followed the general direction of the highway. I could see the road occasionally, and then it would disappear from sight again. The steady hum of traffic in the background reassured me some. I didn't feel so alone knowing that civilization was nearby.

I began to call. "May-beee!" I yelled. Then I paused to listen for his answer. Then I yelled again: "May-beee!"

The only answering sound was the buzz of an angry horsefly that had decided Sheba and I would make a good meal. I swatted at it several times without success.

My stomach was sore again. The extra activity seemed to be making me feel queasy. Thankfully, the dizziness was gone. The last thing I needed was to be dizzy right now!

Sheba and I had covered a mile or so when she came to a sudden stop, causing me to pitch forward in the tippy English saddle.

"Watch it, girl," I scolded.

I gave her a nudge with my heels. Sheba took another step or so, then stopped again. She threw her head up into the air and flared her nostrils. I didn't know Sheba well, but I did understand horse talk. Sheba smelled—or heard—something that was of interest to her.

"I hope it isn't a moose," I muttered, making sure my feet were deep in the stirrups. If Sheba suddenly took off, I wanted to be certain that I went with her.

But Sheba didn't bolt. Instead she neighed loudly and walked forward a few more steps before coming to a stop.

I listened intently, but I didn't hear anything besides the horsefly's whine.

Sheba started forward again, this time at a brisk trot. I pulled her back into a walk, not trusting the rough ground underfoot. "I hope you know what you're doing," I said.

Sheba surged up a little knoll, pulling on the reins.

Her dainty ears swiveled back and forth. I concentrated on keeping my balance. She stopped at the top of the rise and snorted loudly.

Then I heard it! First I heard the peculiar neigh like a horse with a sore throat, followed by *aw-AH-aw*. Only one animal in the world could make a sound like that—a mule! My mule!

Sheba took off down the hill at a lope, her tail arched up over her back. She tossed her head, and I had to saw at the reins to slow her down.

"We're coming, Maybe," I yelled.

Sheba neighed, and an answering bray came back.

It took longer than I expected to actually spot Maybe. Sheba dragged me off the main trail and onto a narrow goat path that crossed an empty streambed. Her head bobbed up and down with every step of her feet, and she snorted loudly several times. She was moving so quickly that I had to duck and dodge the low-hanging bushes that seemed to reach out and grab at me on the narrow path.

I wouldn't even have seen Maybe if he'd have stood perfectly still. His gray coloring blended in perfectly with the gray rocks that surrounded him as he stood in the middle of the dried riverbed. He wasn't on the main trail at all, but off on a little path. Maybe kept braying loudly.

"Maybe!" I hollered excitedly. "I'm coming!"

Then there he was, my handsome mule. He had never looked better to me before. He was a prince, a royal steed, my much-loved horse. And he was alive and well!

Or was he?

Maybe called again, his head held high, but he didn't move toward us.

I knew right then that something was wrong. Maybe had just spent the night alone in the forest. He would want nothing more than come to Sheba and me. But he wasn't moving. Something was wrong. Maybe wouldn't be standing still if he didn't have to.

I got off Sheba and led her along the streambed, avoiding the worst of the rocks. When we were close to Maybe I tied her to a low bush. "Don't pull back," I instructed the horse. I hated tying her with the reins, but I didn't seem to have any choice at the moment. I wanted my hands to be free if I needed to help Maybe.

Maybe bobbed his head excitedly as I got closer, but he still didn't move his feet. A streak of something red, low on his chest, made my heart drop. It looked like blood. The saddle! Was it crooked? Had it slipped and cut into him?

No, everything seemed OK in that way.

Then I was beside Maybe, and I saw the problem. Maybe's front feet were tangled in a heap of rusty barbed wire. Strands of wire curled around his feet, and in one place loops rose as high as his belly. A splintered fence post or two lay curled within the loops of wire. One back foot was free; the other had a single wire snugly wrapped around it. There was one large, angry cut on Maybe's right front leg, up high, almost at chest level.

I could guess what had happened. Maybe, running hard, must have hit the wire, and it had sliced into the top of his leg. Thankfully, mules are smart. While a horse's natural instinct is to panic and struggle, a mule has enough sense to stand still. This instinct had saved Maybe's life.

Before my mom bought Sheba she had owned another Arabian mare. Alli had been a beautiful sorrel brown, and Mom had raced her once or twice successfully. One day they had been exercising in the ditch near our home, and Alli had become tangled up in a discarded heap of barbed wire. The mare had gone crazy and struggled so violently that she ripped both her hind legs to shreds. My mom had been thrown into the edge of the wire but had gotten only minor scratches. Alli wasn't so fortunate. The vet discovered that she had torn tendons and other vital areas, and he had suggested Mom have Alli put down. I was about 4 years old at the time, but I have never forgotten that horrible day.

And now my mule was trapped in barbed wire. I stood there for a moment, just staring at Maybe. What should I do?

Maybe bobbed his head and brayed at me. Get over here and help me! he seemed to be saying.

I quickly hurried to Maybe's head and stroked his shoulder. "Maybe," I gasped, "are you OK?"

Maybe shook his head no.

In spite of my worry I had to smile. That was my cue for Maybe's trick. I'd forgotten about it for a moment, but Maybe hadn't.

"You're a smart boy, aren't you?" I said. I scratched his neck and stepped back so I could see the wire clearer. The cut on Maybe's forearm didn't seem that terrible. It was deep, but the bleeding had stopped. Flies buzzed along the edge of the cut. When I looked closer, I saw several small bloody nicks on Maybe's lower legs. That was all. He wasn't seriously hurt.

But how could I get him out?

I needed a pair of wire cutters. I was sure Auntie Teresa and Uncle James would have some in their barn, but I didn't know where. I wondered what Maybe would do if I rode Sheba back to their place, leaving him behind. Would that make him frantic? Would he struggle to follow us and cut himself worse? I wasn't sure.

If I left Sheba behind to keep Maybe company it would take at least a half hour to get home and another half hour to get back. I didn't know if Maybe could wait that long.

Could I untangle the wire from Maybe's legs without hurting him or myself? I wasn't wearing gloves, and I knew from experience that the sharp hooks on barbed wire can rip skin off bare hands as easily as a knife cuts through butter.

"What should I do?" I asked the mule.

Then I looked up at the sky, and asked Someone who knew the situation better than Maybe or I did. I asked God. "Dear Lord," I prayed, "I've got a big, big problem. Maybe's hurt. He's caught in the wire. What do I do to get him out? Help me know what to do. Help me be brave."

I didn't see an angel, and I didn't hear a voice. But I know that God heard my prayer. I know God heard my prayer because He gave me the courage to try.

"I'll do the best I can," I told Maybe. "Hopefully it will be enough."

I think courage was God's answer to my prayer. John Wayne was right—courage doesn't necessarily mean you aren't afraid. Courage is being afraid, and doing something about it anyway. That's what God did for Maybe and me—He gave me the courage to try.

First I slipped the spare rope around Maybe's head, making a loop around his nose so that I had a makeshift halter. Maybe's bridle was totally gone, probably ripped off by tree branches in his run through the forest.

Then I bent over and looked at Maybe's front feet. The right foot appeared to be the least trapped, so I started there. I carefully grasped a loop of wire and slid it down Maybe's leg. I put the toe of my cowboy boot on the loop to keep it from springing back up his leg, then reached for another coil. When the whole roll was down at the bottom of Maybe's leg, I reached over for Maybe's foot.

"Shake," I said. (That's the cue I use when I ask Maybe to lift his foot to shake it.)

Maybe hesitated. You could almost see him thinking. He had already discovered that any movement caused the barbs to poke him, and he wasn't interested in being hurt.

"Shake, Maybe," I repeated.

Maybe slowly raised his right foot. The coils of wire slid off. One foot was free!

Now a new problem appeared. If I could just take the extra wire and set it somewhere out of our reach we'd be all right. But the wire was wrapped around the old fence posts, and it was apparent that it couldn't be moved very easily. Bits of grass and weeds had grown in, covering some of the wire with fibrous tentacles that wouldn't shift when I pulled. So I had to allow the wire to lay in loose, deadly coils under Maybe's belly.

The horsefly had found Maybe now, and circled him, buzzing loudly. If Maybe even stomped his feet at the horsefly, he could get caught up in the wire again.

"Please don't move, Maybe," I begged. "Not one single, solitary inch."

Now I reached for his left foot. This leg was harder to free. It took me several minutes of wiggling and prying before the leg was loose. And in the process I ripped a chunk of flesh out of the palm of my hand. It wasn't too serious, but it hurt, and I wasn't eager to do it again.

My heart was pounding, and I was panting when I stopped and studied Maybe carefully. I'm not ashamed to admit that I was scared, scared because Maybe's life seemed to be in my hands, and I was so inadequate. If I made a mistake, if Maybe panicked, if I couldn't untangle him, it would be my fault.

Now both of Maybe's front feet were free. Huge rolls of wire lay under his stomach and all around his front feet. But as long as he kept his front feet still, we'd be OK.

The back leg was going to be the hardest. It had only one loop around it, but this loop was twisted and pulled snugly. It was as though Maybe's leg was caught in a wire snare. I was unable to loosen the coil at all. Both ends of the wire were tight and seemed to be fastened into the ground.

Something sharp bit the back of my neck, and I swatted at it. I missed, and watched as the horsefly left me to return to Maybe. Maybe twitched his skin, and the horsefly rose for a minute before settling back on Maybe's belly.

"Stand still, Maybe," I pleaded, swishing the horsefly away. I followed the length of wire down from Maybe's leg, trying to see what was keeping it from moving. There! The wire was stapled into the rotting wooden fence post. And the fence post was caught in the riverbed by piles of rocks and rotting plant material.

I had to reach across the coils of barbed wire, right under Maybe's belly, to reach the fence post. The barbed wire almost seemed alive, and struck at me like a snake. Once there was a rip, and when I looked down at my leg I saw a long tear in my blue jeans.

The wire must have jabbed Maybe, too. I couldn't help but accidentally shift it when I tried to grab the fence post. But Maybe stood as still as a rock. Only his head moved as he watched me with his intelligent brown eyes.

I pulled at the fence post with all my might, but it wouldn't shift.

"Just a few inches," I begged, rearing back and throwing all my weight into it.

Nothing happened.

"OK," I said. "I'll try the other side."

I followed the wire down the other direction and ran into the same problem. This end of the wire was stapled into a second fence post that lay directly under Maybe's hind feet.

You won't be able to understand how afraid this whole process was making me unless you've seen what a horse can do in barbed wire. My biggest fear was that Maybe would panic when I had the wire curled around my hand. He could easily drag me into the wire and under his feet. If Maybe stayed calm and quiet, I'd be OK. If he panicked, I was in big trouble. He had the power to hurt himself and to hurt me, too.

O Lord, help me a little longer. Please!

I pulled on the second fence post, but it too seemed to be glued to the earth. I twisted and wiggled it, but the post wouldn't budge.

"Come on!" I grunted, heaving again and again.

Once I caught my heel on a loop of barbed wire and fell down right behind Maybe. He flinched, his head jerking up, but otherwise didn't move. For once I was truly thankful that I was big and strong. My long arms were able to reach under Maybe, and my extra size meant I had more power. Even so, the fence post didn't move.

I strained against that second post for several minutes until my back began to ache. I was just about to give up when I felt something shift. The staples on the fence post were wiggling loose!

"Yes!" I said, and pulled again.

One staple flew through the air, straight over my back, and landed among the rocks with a tinkle. An inch of slack now appeared in the wire around Maybe's back leg. I reached forward and wrapped the wire around my palm, then pulled again with all my might. At first nothing happened. Then the second staple shot up through the air like a rocket. The wire was free!

My hands shook as I reached between Maybe's hocks and slowly loosened the wire. In a moment or two I had his leg free. My hand throbbed as I very carefully slid the surrounding wires to the side as much as possible, then I asked Maybe to back up.

He took one slow step at a time. Back, and then halt. I slid another bunch of barbed wire out of the way and cued Maybe to back again.

His hind feet were free now! Clusters of wire clung to my pant legs, grabbing with sharp wire teeth, and I carefully pushed them aside. Left foot back, then right foot back. We were almost there . . . We were free!

Maybe took a delicate step forward, feeling with his narrow hooves. He seemed to realize he was out of the wire. He took two fast steps forward, then hesitated. He turned his head back to look at the coils of wire with an angry glare. Then he pranced over to Sheba and snuffled happily. She returned his greeting eagerly.

As the two horses sniffed at each other happily, I bent over and threw up behind the bush. I don't know if it was stress or the flu that made me sick. But I did know one thing: It would be a long time before I complained about being big and strong again. And I wasn't about to complain about Maybe, either. If Maybe hadn't been smart like a mule, and if I hadn't been as strong as a horse, we'd still be trapped in the wire.

The two things that had seemed to be such a problem had suddenly shown me how they could also be an incredible help.

Thank You, God, for helping me! And thank You for knowing what's best.

12

Safe at Last!

I was leading Sheba and Maybe into the barn when Uncle James's car pulled into the driveway. I don't think he saw us at first, because he stopped the car at the house. I saw the car door open, and then it slammed shut again without him getting out. In a moment he drove up beside the barn and staggered out of the car.

"I see someone found Maybe," he said. His face was still pale and his eyes watery.

"You'll never believe what happened—" I started to say, but Uncle James didn't seem to be listening.

"I told you that things would work out," he said. "Someone must have seen your dad's posters."

"But you see—"

"I've been gone for hours!" he complained.

"I found Maybe—"

"Hours!"

"He was in some wire—"

"No one has Gravol!" Uncle James was clearly irritated.

"It was like a snare—"

"The whole town of Nordegg!"

"And Maybe's leg was all tangled—"

Uncle James groaned. "I feel terrible!"

"Uncle James?"

"Not one pill in the entire town. I think I'll climb back into my bed and die in peace!"

"Uncle James!" I was yelling now.

"Put it on my tombstone," James said. "'He died because there was no Gravol!'" Uncle James flopped back in the car and smiled wanly before spinning the car around.

Die in peace? Never! I was going to kill him myself if the flu didn't get him first. I watched him go with my mouth hanging open. I had such an exciting story to tell, and Uncle James didn't even want to hear it!

I put both horses in their stalls, and after quickly unsaddling Sheba, I filled a pail with water for Maybe. He finished the first pail in one big swallow and stomped the floor until I filled the bucket again. After about three buckets of water, he began to beg for something to eat.

"I guess we know who the boss is around here," I muttered, scooping up a gallon of horse cubes. "And it certainly isn't me."

Maybe nodded his head yes as though agreeing with me.

"I don't know how you can be hungry," I told Maybe. "I couldn't eat a thing."

After feeding Maybe and Sheba, I sat down on a bale of straw and closed my eyes. I was so tired. I hadn't gotten much sleep the night before, and today's adventures had just about finished me off. I knew how Uncle James felt. I just wanted to go up to the house and collapse too, but the walk between the barn and the house seemed too far right now.

I must have fallen asleep right there on the bale of straw, because the barn was almost dark when I opened my eyes. At first I wasn't sure where I was. My neck ached (probably from sleeping slumped over on the bales), and my skin was prickly from the straw. I heard voices outside the barn.

"I hope I never see a horse again," someone groaned.

It was my dad!

There was a thump as he slid heavily off the horse, followed by another louder groan.

Mom's voice was soothing as she pulled the barn door open. "Well, you survived, didn't you?" she said.

"If you can call this surviving!" Dad muttered. He reached over and turned the barn light on. "I can tell you, I have blisters on my blisters. My behind feels like—" He stopped midsentence and stared at me. "What are you doing here?" he asked.

"Sarah!" Mom exclaimed. "You're supposed to be in the house, resting."

"We didn't find Maybe," Dad said sadly. "But we will tomorrow, for sure."

"Dad—"

"Don't worry," Dad went on. "I'll do everything I can. I've already promised your mom that I'll ride with her again tomorrow."

Mom raised her eyebrows but didn't say anything.

"Dad—" I tried again, but he interrupted me.

"Maybe can't be far away. In fact, someone told us that there were reports of a mule braying just south of the highway.

"*North* of the highway," Mom corrected.

"South!"

"I'm telling you, Doug, the ranger said they distinctly heard a mule calling north of the highway."

"Dad! Mom!"

"We looked there," Mom said. "We didn't find anything."

"Wait till tomorrow," Dad continued. "We'll find Maybe then, honest. Don't give up, Sarah."

This was my conversation with Uncle James all over again. And there was no way I was going to let my parents stagger back to the house without seeing my surprise. "DAD!" I screamed.

The horses jumped, and my dad finally quit talking.

"Look behind me," I said, moving over.

They both took a step forward, peering through the bars of the stall.

"Maybe?" Mom asked.

"Maybe!" Dad yelled. He began to laugh.

They both ran over and hugged me.

It took a long time to explain what had happened. At first my mom was angry that I had gone out into the forest without them, but by the end of the story her face was calm.

"I won't say you did the right thing," she finally said, "but I do think that God was with you."

Suddenly there was the sound of feet outside the barn door, and Bo appeared around the corner. Auntie Teresa was back! Bo barked happily and loped inside. He jumped up, almost knocking Mom over, and licked her face. Then he saw me and rushed my direction, his tail wagging wildly.

"Get down, dog," I said, raising my arms.

I didn't have anything to worry about. Bo suddenly saw Maybe in the stall behind me and slammed on his brakes. His tail slid between his back legs. He yelped sharply and spun around, raced out the barn door, and disappeared from sight.

Auntie Teresa lead Jesse forward, a big smile on her face. "I bet Maybe's here!" she said happily. She beamed at the mule through the stall bars. "Isn't he a beautiful sight?" she said.

I looked at my mule and smiled. He was beautiful. Even his big jug head and his little stubby tail suddenly seemed beautiful beyond words.

"God answered our prayers," Mom said.

"You don't know the half of it," I sighed.

"God answered my prayers, too," Auntie Teresa said. "Look what I've got." She held out an armload of treasures. "I found your bridle," she told Mom. "And here's the lemonade pitcher." Then she turned to me. "Now, let's see . . . I have your water bottle and a squashed container of suntan lotion," she grinned.

"Thanks," I said, taking the bottles from her. "But what about the Smarties and my bug spray?"

"The Smarties were long gone," Auntie Teresa said. "And I didn't see any bug spray. It must have rolled under a tree."

"I doubt it," I told the group. "I think Mr. Moose was smarter than we realized. He probably kept the bug spray to use when it gets dark!"

After things calmed down my dad passed me his horse's reins. "Here, you take care of this beast," he said. "I'm going to have a long soak in the tub."

"Wait, Doug," Mom called.

He stopped and turned toward Mom. "Actually," he said. "I think I'll have a shower instead. I don't think I could sit in the tub for very long."

I laughed.

"You don't have time for a shower," Mom said slowly. "We should pack up and go home this evening."

"Go home?" Auntie Teresa asked.

Mom nodded her head. "Sarah has school tomorrow," she said.

"School!" I exclaimed. "But I'm sick."

Both Mom and Dad turned and looked at me.

"Get real!" Dad said. "Anyone who's healthy enough to rescue lost horses is healthy enough for school. Go get your suitcase."

I didn't argue. But as I left the barn I could hear my dad complaining. "Drive home tonight?" he whined. "How can I sit for three hours in the truck?"

Mom and Auntie Teresa laughed.

"Stamp collecting," he said. "No one ever gets blisters from stamp collecting."

So I guess that's where my story ends. We took Maybe and Sheba home that evening. Maybe's shoulder wasn't cut too badly, but he and I did have to miss the next endurance race. Mom and Sheba were able to compete, and they won another first-place trophy.

I won't tell you that life has been perfect. I still don't like being this tall, and I still hate it when people call me fat. I think I've quit growing, though, and that's good news to me.

If anyone calls you fat, or skinny, or teases you because you're too big or too small, you need to remember my story. God loves us just the way we are. And sometimes the things we hate the most about ourselves can turn out to be our biggest strengths.

Remember what my friend Carley said: "God doesn't make mistakes."

He didn't make mistakes when He made me, and He didn't make mistakes when He made Maybe. And God didn't make mistakes when He made you, either!